Where the Quaggy Bends

The Quaggy was so creepy and so special there were moments when it was good as being back in the country.

Well, nearly.

Even the Quaggy at its best couldn't compare with what we'd left behind three weeks ago when we moved here. After all, what was the Quaggy? Really it was no more than a gap in the city's city-ness - a musty, weed-choked river winding its way through drab back streets like a wild streak people had forgotten to tame.

Yet Ren seemed to love it.

Also available in Lions

Chris Powling

Where the Quaggy Bends

Lions
An Imprint of HarperCollinsPublishers

First published in Lions 1992

Lions Tracks is an imprint of HarperCollins Children's
Books, a division of HarperCollins Publishers Ltd, 77-85
Fulham Palace Road, Hammersmith London W6 8JB

Printed and bound in Great Britian by HarperCollins
Book Manufacturing Ltd, Glasgow

CHAPTER · ONE

We stood on the edge of the Quaggy, looking down.
So Clint, the kid with the rat's-tail haircut, had to
squint up at us with the sun in his eyes. "Do we
know you?" he asked.

"Maybe," said Ren.

"Do we?" he asked the others.

But they were dazzled by the sun, too. That's
why they didn't rush us, I suppose. They couldn't
be sure how big and nasty we were or even how
many we had in our gang. Trust Ren to have got
us in just the right position.

Not that she'd taken much trouble about it. My
sister's face had the cool, empty look I recognized at
once: her fighting face.

Suddenly, she bent down.

This was a mistake, maybe. It meant they
had their first clear view of her: a stringy, tall-
ish thirteen-year-old too neat and tidy to be
really tough. I saw Clint's eyes widen in surprise, then go hard. "Anyway," he said. "We
know you now..."

"Yeah, " the others smirked. "We know you now."

"... for a bit," Clint said.

"Only a bit?"

Something in Ren's voice stopped him right there —one foot on the bank, the other still in the river. Next to me, I felt Nimi go rigid with fright. "Skip?" she whispered.

"Watch Ren," I said.

We were all watching Ren.

Taking her time, she chose a flattish white pebble from the fistful she'd gathered. As she stood up, she reached behind her. Tucked in the back pocket of her jeans was a catapult.

Just the sight of it —from its wrist-brace to the thickness of its elastic —kept Clint in check. He raised a warning hand to the others.

Trust Ren all right.

"See that petrol can?"

Our heads turned. Half-tilted towards us, the petrol can lay high on the opposite bank, perhaps the length of a cricket-pitch away. From where we were — Ren and Nimi and me, that is — it looked smaller than a baked bean tin. "See it?" she repeated.

"Sure," said Clint.

"Want me to leave my mark on it?"

"That far? Girlie, you won't even reach it."

"Think so?"

"Know so."

"Watch."

She barely took aim. With the wrist-brace in position, the heavy-duty elastic at full stretch and the sight lined up, she simply let fly.

THWOCK!

The sound could have been a pebble smacking into the muddy slope — or into a brick buried deep in the weeds. No way could it have been the denting of a petrol can. Clint sniffed, shaped his lips and sent a gob of spit glinting through the air, up towards us. It flopped on the ground just short of Ren's sneakers. "Missed," he said.

"You reckon?"

"Don't you, girlie? There's no scratch on that can."

"Not on the outside."

"What?"

"Who was aiming at the outside?" my sister said. "No point in spoiling a perfectly good can. I shot through the opening at the top where the lid should be."

"You shot through–"

Clint's mouth hung open a moment, then broadened into a know-all grin. "Nice one, girlie," he said. "You've got plenty of bottle, I'll admit that. But you're three-quarters cuckoo in the brain department."

He jerked a thumb at the ferrety-looking black kid just behind him. "Moxie, suss the can."

"Do we need to, Clint?"

"With this little darlin'," said Clint, "we need to."

"Okay," Moxie shrugged.

He had all our attention as he waded along the Quaggy, sending a V of scummy, curdled water trailing out behind him. So far as we could tell, Ren's pebble hadn't shifted the petrol can one centimetre. In my stomach there was a sudden cold, tight knot of doubt. Was Ren bluffing?

7

Moxie bent over the can, getting a firm grip before he lifted it from the grass. Awkwardly, because it was heavier and muckier than it looked from a distance, he up-ended it at arm's length. We heard a faint rattle as a white pebble fell out, bounced at his feet and rolled down the slope to the river where it plopped out of sight.

Everyone gasped, I swear.

Except Ren.

Her gaze was where it had been all the time — on the kid with the rat's tail haircut. Clint's grin had frozen to his face. "Good... good shot," he managed to say.

"I meant it to be," said Ren.

"We'll..."

"Yes?"

"...be going, then."

"Fine."

Clint seemed about to say more, but thought better of it. Instead, with a gesture like a frontier-scout getting a wagon train on the move, he hustled the others away. They were still staring back over their shoulders at Ren, or at her catapult, as they splashed through the shallows after their leader. Level with the petrol-can, one of them stopped to pick up something small and white from the water. His words carried back to us as he showed the others. "She *did* get a direct hit. See? From naffin' miles away!"

"A fluke," someone suggested.

"Yeah? Looked like a naffin' fluke an' all..."

Even as the Quaggy's greenery swallowed them up, they were still arguing about it.

Ren spoke first. "Not bad," she said softly. "For

a little darlin', that is. For a girlie..."

"Not bad?" Nimi gasped. "It was brilliant — *brilliant*! Where did she learn to shoot like that?"

"She taught herself," I said. "Out in the woods. She was always practising. Every minute, practically. Right, Ren?"

Ren didn't answer. She was still staring along the Quaggy, a faraway look in her eyes. "What's up, Ren?" I asked.

"Nothing."

"You looked like you wished you'd gone with them."

"Do I?"

"Yes," I said. "You do."

"With them?" exclaimed Nimi. "Ren wants to go with them? They're manky, they are. Always looking for trouble — beating kids up, doing damage an' suchlike. Everyone round here knows Clint and his mates. Why would your sister want to go with them?"

"Ask her," I said.

Nimi shook her head. She was too shy ever to speak to Ren directly. Sometimes it really got me down having to pass on her comments and queries.

Not that it bothered Ren. She seemed to think it was funny. "Thrills," she told Nimi. "That's why."

"Clint and his gang are *thrilling*?" I snorted.

"Them and the Quaggy, Skip. I like the Quaggy. It's creepy and... and special."

I knew what she meant. The Quaggy was so creepy and so special there were moments when it was as good as being back in the country.

Well, nearly.

Even the Quaggy at its best couldn't compare with

9

what we'd left behind three weeks ago when we moved here. After all, what was the Quaggy? Really it was no more than a gap in the city's city-ness — a musty, weed-choked river winding its way through drab back streets like a wild streak people had forgotten to tame.

Yet Ren seemed to love it.

Now, for instance. Her eyes glinted with excitement. "Nimi," she said. "Where's the scariest part of the Quaggy?"

"Me?" Nimi squeaked. "You're asking me?"

"Why not? You've always lived here, haven't you? It's Skip and me who are new."

"The *scariest* part?"

"Right."

As usual, Nimi's look was on me rather than my sister. I saw her thinking furiously. "I reckon..."

"Yes?"

"I reckon it's where the kid got drowned."

"Drowned?" I said. "What — in the Quaggy?"

Nimi nodded. "Last summer, Skip."

"Must've been a pretty dim kid to snuff it in six inches of water. Poisoned, I *could* believe."

"The kid drowned, Skip. That's definite. But not here — along where the Quaggy's deeper. Ask anyone."

"Who was the kid?" Ren asked.

Nimi shuddered and looked away. This wasn't her favourite subject we could tell. "Some... some kid who lived near here," she said.

"Could you take us to where it happened?"

"Now?"

"Now," said my sister. "Okay, Skip?"

"Okay by me."

"You really want to go there?" pleaded Nimi.

Ren and I glanced at each other. Why not? Having seen off Clint and his mob, we'd got nothing better to do with the afternoon. "Assuming this dead kid stuff is true," said Ren. "And not just a story..."

That was enough for Nimi. She started at once.

Trailing her wasn't easy, though.

Somehow she drifted through the leafiness and the water as if she were no more solid than a ghost. Was she truly eleven — the same age as me? She seemed so small, so thin... so quick.

Really quick.

Even Ren was left breathless trying to keep up with her. Well, fairly breathless. For Ren, keeping up meant flitting from one side of the Quaggy to the other as high as the fences and trees that screened us off from the traffic. The stinky, non-stop traffic. Nearly as good as the country, did I say?

I must've been mad.

Ren herself wouldn't go that far. It's always fun to explore new territory — like pirates hotfooting it after treasure. But here? Amongst this junkyard messiness?

Not that I could complain it wasn't private. All round us was tough, wiry scrub with a mesh of branches overhead so dense the sky seemed to beam down shadows rather than sun. I felt my shirt sticking to my back and sweat prickle in my hair. Up in front, Nimi turned and looked back. "Where's Ren?" she asked.

"Ren?"

"Has she got lost?"

I swung round. "She's fetching more stones for

11

her catapult, I expect. No good running out of ammo. Not when Clint's lot might be tracking us."

Nimi shook her head. "Not to this place, Skip. Kids steer clear of this place."

"Why?"

"They just do."

"Always?"

"Except for a dare, maybe."

"Because they're scared of drowning, too?"

Nimi hesitated. "More like... bad luck. As if they might catch bad luck."

"From a place?"

"Wait till you see it," Nimi said.

"Is it close?"

"Pretty close."

"Better get a move on, then."

"Without Ren?"

"Why not? How far behind can she be? She's bound to turn up sooner or later."

"You sure, Skip?"

"Look," I said. "We don't need Ren to hold our hands every step of the way. At least, I don't. Suppose she got lost? Or fed up with the whole idea? We could be hanging about for the rest of the afternoon. She's not our flippin' keeper, is she?"

"No," Nimi said.

"So?"

Nimi took another look back along the Quaggy. Already it seemed dark and risky and Ren-less. Especially Ren-less. I licked my lips. "So?" I repeated.

"Okay," she said. "Let's go."

It wasn't far at all. As the Quaggy got wider, its banks began to flatten and spread themselves but there were still plenty of brambles for us to step over

12

or duck under. When Nimi came to a halt I was concentrating so hard on not being snagged I almost cannoned into her. "Are we there?" I asked.

She pulled aside a last tangle of leaves. "See, Skip?"

"Yeah," I said.

Here was the place all right. Here the river really was a river.

Curving so sharply it seemed to turn back on itself, the Quaggy took on a completely new look. This was just the spot for a sudden splash followed by screaming, floundering panic —probably over there in the shadow of the blocked-up sewer pipe. Would it take two minutes to drown? Three maybe? I felt phantom water slosh in my stomach. "Who did you say this kid was?" I asked, hoarsely.

"Who knows?" Nimi shrugged.

13

"Didn't he realize it was dangerous here?"

"Couldn't have done."

"Or didn't care," I said. "Some kids wouldn't care."

"No?"

"Ren wouldn't, for instance."

"Wouldn't she? What about rat's pee disease, Skip — you know, that illness you get from swimming in bad water?"

"Wouldn't worry my sister," I boasted. "Go snorkelling here, Ren would. Or deep-Quaggy-diving. Probably she'd get in a bit of underwater target practice with her catapult, too, just to keep her eye in."

"Bound to, yes."

I shot her a look. Was Nimi teasing me?

Not that I could see.

She was staring at the bend in the river — or was it across the river? My eyes followed the direction of hers. On the far bank, almost lost between reedy water and overhanging branches, was a house.

At least, I assumed it was a house.

I'd have missed it altogether if the slant of the afternoon sun hadn't picked out a crumbling verandah and the slope of a roof. Was it some kind of sports pavilion? Or a boarded-up bandstand? "What a weird place," I said. "It's about as close to the Quaggy as it can get without actually falling in. Who owns it, Nimi?"

"No idea."

"Is it empty?"

"Don't think so."

"How can you tell from here?"

"Listen."

14

"What?"

"Listen..." Nimi said.

Then I heard the music, too.

Don't ask me what was so unearthly about it. It was only some soppy song, after all.

"Sally, Sally - don't ever wander
Away from the alley and me...
Sally, Sally... marry me, Sally.
And happy forever I'll be."

The thin, sharp voice reminded me of old movies on television — the kind Dad only allowed us to waste time on when we were ill. Ren called them fogey-films. No soundtrack was ever this scratchy, though. No record-player, either. "It's a gramophone," I said. "An ancient, wind-up gramophone."

"When skies are blue you're beguiling
And when they're grey you're still smiling... smiling."

Dimly, uncannily, the song drifted across to us as the light behind the trees faded and the whole scene dissolved into a clip from a fogey-film.

"Sally, Sally — pride of our alley,
You're more than the whole world to me."

Suddenly the music stopped.

For a moment it was as if every sound in the universe had been switched off with it. Then, bit by bit, noise returned: our own breathing, the thin twitter of birds, the sweep and hush of the river.

The house had slipped so far back into the gloom,

15

I might have missed it altogether if I hadn't seen it already. "Who lives there?" I asked. "And how do they get down to it? Some path on the other side?"

"Probably."

"They must know about the drowning," I said.

"What?"

"The people who live in the house."

"You reckon?"

"Happened within ear-shot, didn't it?"

"They could've been out. Or on holiday."

"Yeah... unless the kid himself lived here."

Nimi shook her head. "They'd never have stayed, Skip. Not when it happened right on their doorstep. No one could bear it. They'd *have* to move somewhere else..."

"If they could, you mean. Who'd buy a house like this? I bet it's damp from cellar to chimneypot — not to mention the bad press it must've got. It might even be haunted."

"Haunted?"

"By the dead kid."

Nimi stared at me, wide-eyed. I didn't blame her — by now I was spooking myself.

So we were in just the right mood to jump out of our skins.

It was the crack that did it — a crack like a stepped-on twig with a flurry of leaves to cover it up. Fifty metres — maybe thirty — to our left. Slowly, hardly daring to breathe, we sank to a crouch. Neither of us spoke.

SNAP! *Shush...*

This time it was further off and in a different direction altogether. From the water's edge came a whirr of wings as a pair of drab city waterfowl took to

16

the air, squawking with rage. What had disturbed them? Were we surrounded already? "Nimi," I hissed. "I thought you told me..."

"Skip, it's true. Clint never comes here. None of them do."

"Till now, you mean."

"Reckon they've spotted us?"

I laughed bitterly. "They'd be closing in for the kill if they had."

Even new kids like me were fully clued-up about Clint. His dad owned a video-shop, and it was said Clint sampled every tape for himself — especially the tough guy ones. He had a knife which he called his Little Friend. He'd hold it to your throat while you read him a story —from a book that was upside down. You were only allowed one mistake.

How could I avoid that mistake?

Signalling Nimi to copy me, I pressed myself flat to the ground. "Crawl," I whispered.

"On our hands and knees?"

"Is there any other way to crawl?"

"But how far, Skip?"

"Till we're clear of this place at least. D'you fancy Clint catching you just where the Quaggy gets serious? Later we can run for it, maybe. Let's go."

I slithered forward, trying to ignore the dank, earthy smell in my nostrils.

It was awful.

Before I'd covered ten metres, sweat was running into my eyes, my knees and elbows were scuffed raw and one of my fingers was bleeding. Doggedly I forced myself on —one metre more, one metre more, one metre more. I felt as if I were dragging the track along with me. Each leg was like a ton weight — a dead weight at that. Was I getting a stitch in my side now? Don't stop, Skip. Don't stop...

Stupid, of course.

Eventually, as much from boredom as bruises, I collapsed face downwards and lay still.

Beneath me, I felt the whole world spin. Was Nimi just as worn out? I swivelled and looked back.

She sat cross-legged in the middle of the path, grinning.

Grinning?

I rolled over and propped myself up. Between Nimi and me, in the crook of a tree, was Ren. She was grinning, too. "Hi, Skip!" she called. "I've been testing this catapult of mine..."

She lifted it, sighted it and let go.

SNAP! *Shush... shush... shush...*

In the undergrowth behind me, I head a commotion of phoney Clints on the move. "Good, eh?" said Ren. "Nothing like a sound-effect to build up the tension. Er... if you don't mind me saying so, Little Bruv, you look a teeny bit rumpled. What have *you* been testing, I wonder?"

And she winked at Nimi.

At Nimi of all people.

Can you blame me for my instant mega-sulk?

CHAPTER · TWO

"She reckoned it was funny, Dad," I complained.

"And was it?"

"Not for me."

Dad frowned and scratched his bald spot. "How about Nimi?"

I hesitated. Nimi always laughed at Ren's jokes. Also at mine, admittedly. In this case, she'd giggled all the way home. "It was different for Nimi," I said. "She didn't come close to ripping her finger off."

"Uh-huh."

I hated it when Dad did his uh-huh act on me. It was nearly as bad as when he said nothing at all—just peered at me over his spectacles. "Look," I sighed, "are you going to tell Ren off or not?"

"What sort of things shall I say?"

"Sorry?"

"Well, there's plenty I could say. Keep clear of the Quaggy, for instance. Or stay away from Clint. Or be nice to your little brother..."

"Forget it," I said.

"Then again, there's that catapult of hers. I'm a

bit bothered about that catapult..."

Now came his spectacle-peering.

I shifted awkwardly. This conversation was taking a turn I didn't like. "It's not illegal," I reminded him. "Ren checked with the police..."

"I know."

"And they told her a catapult doesn't count as an offensive weapon. Not like a gun, or a dagger or a swordstick..."

"I know, Skip."

"Besides, Ren never points it at anything *living*. It's a point of principle, she says."

"I'm sure it is," said Dad, drily.

"You can trust her, Dad," I promised. "I've never seen Ren even threaten to use it. And she's such a smart shot you'd have to be a nutcase to take her on."

"So what happens when she comes up against a nutcase?"

I couldn't answer that. "Hey," I said. "Are we talking about Ren or are we talking about me?"

"You," said Dad. "Sorry. So what do you want me to do?"

"Nothing," I said.

"Hold on, Skip. A moment ago you seemed to have a real grievance. I'd better do *something* hadn't I?"

"No," I insisted. "I've changed my mind."

"You sure?"

"Positive."

Dad nodded and smiled.

Even worse, it was a Ren-type smile. "I bet you write about it, though," I said.

Dad was always putting Ren and me into his

books. Not so as we'd be recognized, of course, just snippets of talk and odd happenings we'd never noticed at the time till we were reminded of them as we read. Having a dad who's a children's author can be a real pain. "Why don't you write stories for grown-ups?" I once said to him.

"Because I like stories better than I like grown-ups," he'd replied.

I ask you, what kind of answer was that?

At the top of the stairs to his workroom, I stopped a moment by the landing window. Outside, darkness was gathering but the sky was so overcast it could have been midnight already. Rain had been falling steadily ever since we got home. Some summer.

And some place.

Gloomily, I looked over the sodden gardens and shadowy backyards towards the endless flickering of headlights up and down Vandyke Hill. Could I really feel our floorboards tremble as a train rattled its way across the embankment to one side of us? And was it true the shop-signs in the precinct opposite would blink on-and-off now, on-and-off now, right through till morning?

I'd never get used to the city.

Or the Quaggy.

For the Quaggy was out there, too. Rain would be whispering in the leaves along its banks, would be glinting in the water where it swept around the sewer-pipe, would be tap-tap-tapping on the shutters of the hidden house.

I shuddered.

Pull yourself together, Skip. Licked by a little thing like embarrassment? Not you, kid. For a start,

21

you must get even with Ren.

How, though?

An apple-pie bed, maybe? Setting her alarm-clock to go off at 2.00.am? Soot on her tooth-brush?

I shook my head. Baby-ish stuff like that would just make it worse. Besides, I'd played those tricks on her before. What I really wanted to do was make my sister CRINGE... the way I did when I remembered her grin as she perched in the tree.

SNAP! *Shush...*

Ugh.

So why was it, undressing for bed, I couldn't crank my brain into action? For once, even the half-darkness of my bedroom didn't keep me awake, not to mention my skinful of scratches. The instant my head hit the pillow, I fell asleep.

I'd have snored on till breakfast if Ren hadn't had other ideas. "Skip," she shook me.

"Whaa... ?"

"Skip? It's me."

"Huh?"

"Me, you bozo. Wake up."

"Ren?"

"No, Dracula. Come on, Little Bruv — shift yourself. We'll miss her if you don't get a move on."

"Her? You mean..."

"Got it in one. It's the news-report."

Already I'd swung my legs out of bed and was feeling for my slippers. Where were they? Stuff them. I'd go barefoot. Ren would be halfway there by now.

Further, actually. By the time I'd caught up with her, she was huddled on the stairs that led down to the living-room, her face tight against the bannisters.

Below, in a world of his own, was Dad.

Also below, in a world of her own — the oblong world of television—was Mum. The title-music faded under her voice:

"… not a pretty sight. Here violence, and the effects of violence, are a matter of routine. The victims have suffered so much they can't afford to care any more. And it's an open question whether those responsible ever cared in the first place…"

Her voice, cool and crisp, spelled out facts I didn't know about a place I'd never heard of. Next came footage of bombings and gunfire and a landscape so smashed up it made no sense. "A bewilderness," Mum called it.

Ren and I blinked and stared.

Of course, we'd have liked more of Mum. There were too many shots where she wasn't on camera, wasn't talking even. Often the story seemed to be coming over without any help from her at all but at the finish, as the music faded up and the credits rolled, we saw her name in the usual big letters. By then we'd finished our counting. "Six," I said.

"Five," Ren insisted.

We meant the number of times during the programme Mum had flicked back her hair. This had become her trademark. Once, when Mum had forced herself not to do it, she'd been snowed under with letters from viewers protesting that the flick was part of her personality and they liked it — so please bring it back. I nodded agreement. "Okay, five. That last one was only half a flick."

Although there was nothing more to see on the

channel, we knew Dad would sit tight on for ages, his eyes on the blank screen. Very handy for helping us slip back upstairs.

At the door of my bedroom, Ren caught my arm. "Skip, can I come in a sec?" she asked. "For a chat?"

"What about?"

"Oh... nothing much."

"Sure," I said.

I was trying not to smirk. She wanted to say sorry, obviously. With Ren that could take quite a while.

I settled back on my bed. Ren stood at the window, gazing out. The rain had stopped at last. There was even some moonlight — unless that was city electrics, too. At any rate, I could see my sister's face outlined against the glass. It was so much like Mum's I almost gasped out loud. As if she'd read my mind, she said "One day I'll do the same job as her, Skip. Or something like it."

"You bet," I said.

"Except I'll take my kids with me. Everywhere I go."

"They won't let you, Ren."

"Who won't?"

"Them. The people in charge. They just won't. Too dangerous, they'll say. Also it'll muck up things like exams and stuff."

"Yeah? Well stuff exams, Skip. That's what I'll say."

I gave a shrug. "They still won't let you. They'll put your kids in a home. Or find someone to look after them the way Dad looks after us."

"My kids' dad will come as well," said Ren. "We'll share what we do — sometimes the danger, sometimes the looking after."

"Couldn't our mum and dad do that?" I asked. "Take turns, I mean?"

"You reckon, Skip?"

"No," I said.

"Neither do I."

We both laughed. The thought of Dad taking Mum's place was as wild as the notion of Mum taking Dad's. Or me taking Ren's.

"Skip?" she said.

"Yes?"

"Tell me about Nimi. Okay, is she?"

"Nimi?"

"For a friend, I mean."

"Fine," I said.

So that's what she was leading up to. After three weeks of hero-worship Ren's one-kid Fan Club had finally got on her nerves. Sad, really, but I wasn't surprised. "Good," said Ren. "I've been hoping you'd hit it off with her."

"What?"

"Well, you have been sort of mopey since we moved to the city. That's why I've gone around with you so much. But now you've got a good mate like Nimi maybe I can... you know... strike out by myself a bit."

"By yourself?" I said, sitting up.

"That's right, Skip. I mean, it's time I made my own friends, isn't it? And leave you to make yours — people like Nimi and such. You're not upset, are you?"

"No."

"I am three years older than you, remember."

"Two-and-three-quarters."

25

"Okay, okay. The point is that Nimi's exactly your age."

"A week younger."

"Almost perfect," said Ren. "Right?"

"Right."

"So you won't mind too much if I go my own way after this? Seeing you've got Nimi for company?"

I cleared my throat. "No problem."

Even across the room, with the fuss of night traffic roaring in my ears, I heard Ren's sigh of relief. "That's great," she said. "Skip, I'm really glad we've had this talk. It's been quite a worry that you wouldn't understand what I was getting at. Should've known better, shouldn't I? See you around, then. Cheers, Little Bruv."

"Cheers," I said.

But I don't suppose she heard me because I'd buried my head under the duvet.

CHAPTER · THREE

"Is it my fault?" Nimi asked next day.

"No."

"You're sure, Skip?"

"Course."

"Because I'll drop out if you want me to. You and Ren can go around by yourselves again like you did in the country. I mean, I'll still be seeing you, won't I?"

She looked almost as upset as I felt. This wasn't why I shook my head, though. More the possibility of the long, summer holidays without her *or* Ren. "Forget it, Nimi," I growled. "It's just between me and my sister. Nothing to do with you. What makes you think you're that important?"

"I don't," said Nimi.

"Good."

Irritably, to give myself a breather, I lowered both bags of shopping onto the pavement — and felt a pang of guilt as Nimi did the same with the other two. After all, she was helping me carry them home.

Not that I was taking her out of her way. We had

the same address, almost — though the bare basement flat next door which Nimi shared with her mother and her big brother, Ravinder, felt worlds apart from the four floors-worth of books, papers, pictures and oddments where we lived. I sometimes thought our city house was simply our country house tipped up on end.

I bent to pick up the bags again. Nimi bent, too. "I saw your mother on the telly last night," she said shyly.

"That late?"

"I was sitting up with Mum. She gets lonely with Ravi off on his trip to India. I thought she was really good — your mother, I mean."

"Always is."

"Aren't you afraid she'll..."

"Get killed?"

"Or hurt," Nimi said quickly.

I smiled wryly. Mum never let anyone mention the risks she took with her job. If ever you brought it up she'd do her famous hair-flick, point a loaded finger straight at your heart and pretend to gun you down for being such a wimp. " Of course we're afraid," I said. "Dad says he permanently holds a bit of his breath in case something happens to her. It's a family catch-phrase. But that's how it's been with Mum right from the beginning. You get used to it. Besides, she's incredibly lucky. Like Ren."

"She is," Nimi agreed. "They're a dead spit of each other."

"Think so?"

"And like you, of course."

"Of course," I said.

Really I took after Dad — too much imagination.

28

Wasn't that why I'd made such a nerd of myself yesterday? Scaredycat Skip, the Snap-Shush kid?

We walked in silence for a while, not taking our second breather till we reached the point where the High Street crossed the Quaggy. On either side of the road now were the cast-iron railings of a bridge — in my opinion a bridge much too fancy for a neighbourhood like ours.

"Hey," said Nimi suddenly. "I can hear people down there."

"In the river?"

"It's Clint and Co., I think."

Cautiously we peered over the ironwork making sure we couldn't be seen. By now Nimi had briefed me on who-was-who so I recognized their voices for myself: Clint, the leader; Moxie, his lieutenant; Johnny Chan whose dad ran the local takeaway and Olive from the children's home halfway up Vandyke Hill. A full gang-gathering apparently. "Ren's down there, too," Nimi said.

"Ren?"

"Further along the river, see? Isn't that her yellow T-shirt? She's coming this way."

"Towards Clint?"

"He hasn't seen her yet — and she hasn't seen him as far as I can tell."

"Nimi, we've got to warn her!"

"How, Skip?"

I saw what she meant.

Shouting out would tell Clint exactly where Ren was... also where we were, loaded down with carrier bags. But if we dumped them to help Ren they'd vanish at once sure as the city was the city. "We're snookered," I groaned.

Helplessly, we watched what was going on below.

Ren was wading in mid-river, kicking up spray as she came till her jeans and T-shirt must have been soaked.

Beneath us, the voices died away.

Then Clint appeared. With a toss of his rat's-tailed head, he mooched out from the arch of the bridge and sploshed his way upstream, trailed by Moxie, Olive and Johnny Chan. "Is it a meeting?" Nimi asked.

"A show-down, probably."

"It doesn't look that way, Skip."

Nimi was right. As Clint and Ren approached each other, they lifted their fists in salute like blood-brothers. Clint held out a hand palm-upwards. Ren smacked it hard with hers — the crack of skin on skin so sharp it echoed along the Quaggy. The rest of the gang circled round her as she repeated the hand-slaps with each of them: crack-crack, crack-crack, crack-crack.

Next came another blood-brother salute.

Finally, all five kids waded slowly to the bank through the knee-high water, clambered up the slope and disappeared into the trees.

The leaves shifted back into place behind them.

At last I could speak. "Well," I said. "There's Ren fixed up for the next six weeks. With her new pal, Clint. That's why she slipped away yesterday — to set this up."

"Skip, it may be a... sort of trick."

"A trick?"

"Yes..."

"Sort of?"

She winced. If my voice sounded the way I felt, I

didn't blame her. "I'll tell you what sort of a trick it is, Nimi," I snarled. "It's a dirty trick. Ren wanted to team up with those creeps all along. So why not say so? Instead, she gave me all that Big Sister Guff. She was ashamed to tell the truth so she dressed it up as if it was all about me being *younger*. That was the trick."

Nimi said nothing.

The Quaggy was empty and quiet now — dreary, too, as if all yesterday's colour had been crushed out of it by today's multi-ton slab of sky. Honestly, who'd settle for a tip like this?

Me, that's who.

Where else in the city was there? And what more had the holidays to offer? Dad was sinking deeper and deeper into his new book and Mum's next visit wasn't due till the autumn so how could I just step back like a good Little Brother and hand the Quaggy over to Ren?

Besides...

I felt an idea taking shape.

... besides, if Nimi could be trusted, wasn't there one stretch of the river we were bound to have to ourselves? It would be scary, of course. But wasn't everything scary in the city? According to Ren, that was the thrill of it. So why not show her I could cope, too — even if I was two-and-three-quarter years younger?

Not on my own, though.

Casually, I licked my lips. "Fancy a bit of exploring tomorrow?" I asked.

"Exploring, Skip?"

"Down the Quaggy."

"The Quaggy?"

"An investigation, that's all," I said. "Who knows what we might turn up?"

Nimi's face told me she'd guessed already which part of the Quaggy I had in mind. In a voice so small she seemed to be talking to herself rather than me, she said "Okay, Skip. If it's what you really want..."

CHAPTER · FOUR

Again I checked my watch. Had we really been here only ten minutes? I twisted to get the crick out of my neck. "You all right?" I asked.

Nimi nodded. "Fine."

She didn't look fine. She looked scared stiff.

Even from the slope, with the house between us and the bend in the Quaggy, it was hard to forget the drowning. "This rain's enough to get anyone down," I said. "Funny that. Listening to Dad, you'd never guess it rains in the Quaggy."

"Your dad talks about the Quaggy?"

"You bet. Knows it from when he was a kid. Actually, he *only* knows it from when he was a kid. In those days the Quaggy was different: you could skate on it in winter, go boating in summer and catch fish in it all the year round, practically. According to him, that is. He's a writer, remember. What they says doesn't have to be true."

"Doesn't it?"

"It has to be better than true."

"Better?"

"So Dad reckons."

Nimi frowned. "His books are better than true, Skip. Not always nicer, though. And he's never mentioned the Quaggy."

"Yet," I said.

The house seemed odder than ever from this side. I could imagine spooky cricketers, gloved and padded up, clumping down the broad steps from the front door. Or a cobwebby brass-band spread right along the verandah playing show-tunes. But who would be listening here in the Quaggy? And where would the batsmen find a pitch? "It's a kind of hermit-house," said Nimi. "Do hermits play old wind-up gramophones, Skip?"

"This one does."

Nimi shivered. "I could do with a tune right now."

"Like what?"

"Anything, so long as it's cheerful."

"Look," I said. "You don't have to stay."

"Do you want me to?"

"Please yourself."

To my relief, she just sighed. Whatever my next move was, I wanted Nimi there when I made it.

Eventually, even I couldn't stall any more. "Shall we..."

"Okay, Skip."

We crept forward bush-by-bush. All I could hear was rain and footsteps — plus... once or twice, a flurry of jogged leaves. My footsteps, that is, and leaves jogged by me. As usual, Nimi seemed to drift along weightlessly.

Crossing the track we edged up the verandah steps. As they sagged under our weight, Nimi's wish for a tune was granted. We recognized the spindly,

34

girlish voice at once.

"Little old lady passing by
Catching everyone's eye.
You have such a charming manner sweet and shy
Little old bonnet set in place
And a smile on your face
You're a perfect picture in your lavender and lace."

I was reminded of faded photographs in dusty albums. I glanced back up the dirt path. The traffic swishing the trees at the other end of it seemed a million miles away. I lifted the knocker quickly and let it fall. "Anyone home?" I called.

No answer.

Twice more I knocked before pressing my ear flat against the front door. Someone was coming.

Shuffle, shuffle, shuffle—thud.

What?

Shuffle, shuffle, shuffle—thud.

The woodwork rattled and an old-fashioned lock clicked back. Slowly, judderingly, the door itself began to move. Behind me, Nimi gave a gasp.

I could see why.

The man who stood in the opening was ancient enough to be eerie. He looked so frail I wondered whether his walking-frame was there to prop him up or weigh him down in case a sudden draught blew him away. His breath hissed through the loosest and yellowest false teeth I've ever seen. "What's your business?" he asked. His deep voice made us jump — somehow it hadn't shrivelled like the rest of him.

"Um... sorry to disturb you," I said. "But–"

"Children? Are you children?"

"Er... yes, sir."

He bent towards us, peering ahead with watery eyes. "Can't see you in this light. Stand forward a bit. What are you after, then? Money? Mischief?"

I stayed where I was.

I felt Nimi edge closer. Was this for her protection or mine? What was I supposed to say next? When the words finally came they even took me by surprise. "Bob-a-Job," I blurted out.

"What's that?"

"We're doing Bob-a-Job."

"You're wolf-cubs?"

"Scouts," I said.

"And you still do Bob-a-Job? Scouts did Bob-a-Job when I was a lad. Thought they'd given it up years ago. How much do you charge these days?"

"Fifty pence," I said. "A pound if the job's really tough."

"Really tough, eh?"

"Tell us what you want done, sir, and we'll give you an estimate."

"An estimate?"

Something had gone wrong with his breathing. It still went in-and-out, but it was more complicated now. I took a moment to realize what had happened. He was laughing.

Then he was choking.

For the first time, I noticed the cigarette in his hand. No wonder his teeth were yellow. So were his fingers. Even his wispy grey hair had a yellowish, nicotine tint. "Is he okay?" Nimi whispered.

"Smoker's cough," I said.

As the old man struggled to get his breath, more

ash spilled over his trousers and baggy cardigan. It looked like bits of him — as if, without his clothes and walking-frame to hold him together, he'd fall apart, wrinkle-by-wrinkle. We stared, fascinated. "You still there?" he asked suddenly.

"Sir?"

"Thought my cough might've sent you packing. Not popular nowadays, smokers."

"Okay with us, sir."

"And you still want a job?"

"Do we?" I asked Nimi.

Her eyes were still on the old man.

Behind him, the music had stopped. It was an old wind-up gramophone, definitely. I caught the brief rr-rr-rr of its needle at the end of the record before the motor ran down. "Er... what sort of job is it?" I asked.

He flicked what was left of the cigarette out into the rain. "Better come in and see."

"Nimi?"

"You first, Skip."

But it was the old man who went first, huddled over his frame like a thin, grey spectre too feeble to be frightening and too stubborn to fade away. I hung back, lowering my voice. "It'll be okay, Nimi," I told her. "Dad's written a story about Bob-a-Job so I know all about it. We'll finish as fast as we can and split the fifty pence between us."

"Skip, we mustn't."

"Why not?"

"Because he thinks we're real scouts."

"So what?"

"But it's not true, Skip."

"Can't it be better than true?" I snapped.

37

Turning my back on her, I stepped indoors.

All round me were piles of furniture, tea-chests and shapes-under-dustsheets clearly dumped long ago by removal men and never touched since.

That still left plenty of space.

Somehow the huge, square room managed to be cluttered and empty both at once. There wasn't a scrap of homeliness anywhere apart from a table, a footstool and the gramophone, grouped round an ancient iron stove near the French doors opposite.

Moving at his shuffle-shuffle pace the old man had almost reached them. We watched as he manoeuvred the walking-frame into just the right position for getting up again then lowered himself gingerly into the chair. His eyelids fluttered and began to close, then blinked open again as he remembered us. "You youngsters still with me?"

"Yes, sir."

I crossed the room towards him. Only something ridiculous, like the old man sprouting vampire-teeth, would have stopped me now.

He didn't look that bad.

Weird, though.

Lit from behind by the French doors, the curve of his head was skull-like while over his shoulder, through the rain-swept glass, the bend in the Quaggy gave him a moody, drowned-kid backdrop that sent a shiver down my spine. "Cold, are you?" he asked.

"No."

"I am. Never warm, nowadays. Can't keep a fire going all summer, though. It's bad for you."

"Is it?"

He glared at me suspiciously. "Of course it is. It makes you soft. Surprised you don't know that—being a boy scout. Where's your uniform, son? Don't you do Bob-a-Job in uniform any more? Always used to."

"Not any more," I said. "We try to keep our uniforms clean for... for church parades."

"That so?"

He didn't seem convinced. Cocking his head, he looked at me doubtfully. "Are you a machine-minded kid?" he asked. " Good at this High Tech business?"

"High Tech?" I said.

He nodded at the gramophone. "Not Low Tech like this. Seen one of these, have you? It's a Columbia Grafanola. Very smart and up-to-date when it first came out."

"When was that, sir?"

"Don't ask me. I got it donkey's years ago and it

was second-hand then. Do you know how it works?"

"Batteries?"

I knew that would make him laugh. He was still wheezing as he beckoned us closer to the table. "Watch."

I suppose he was showing off a bit. The way he flipped off the old 78 record, put it carefully into a cardboard sleeve marked "A.B. Music Stores, 386 York Road, Wandsworth" and added it to a pile beside his chair, made him seem years younger. About eighty, maybe.

The gramophone looked much the same age. It was a black oblong box with a lid hinged on one side, a red felt turntable and chrome fittings that included a little metal pouch for needles. While he put on another record, he folded the needle-arm back on itself as if leaning it on its elbow. "Would you like to see how it operates?" he asked.

He was itching to show us, I could tell. "Please, sir."

"Here goes, then."

He wound it with a small handle at the front, slipped a catch on the turntable, straightened the needle-arm and lowered it on to the record. At once there was a hard, brittle crackling before violins and a piano took over. Then came the voice:

"'I don't understand some boys,'
Says Suzie, growing wild.
'They seem to think they know it all
And treat me like a child.
For instance, Archibald.
Well, you know Archibald....'"

40

The old man was sitting back now, his face cracked into a broad, false-teeth smile.

> *"When nights are damp and chilly*
> *It sleets and hails and snows,*
> *If he says "Ain't it close tonight?"*
> *What Archibald says goes.*
> *If passing through the country*
> *He sees a flock of crows,*
> *When he tells me they're nightingales,*
> *What Archibald says goes..."*

Beaming, tapping his foot, he asked. "What do you think?"

"Great," I said.

"It's fun," added Nimi.

This was true.

Listening to the record reminded me of thumbing through old newspapers for a school project — or picking up some object in an antique shop and feeling the touch of other fingers from other times before it became historical. Except this relic was so *perky.*

> *"When dining off a chicken*
> *He sees the parson's nose,*
> *If he says it's t'other end*
> *What Archibald says goes."*

It was obvious why the singer, whoever she was, cheered the old man up. A group called The Beatles did the same for Mum and Dad — Mum in particular. She played their songs endlessly. It was one of the signs that she was home.

41

Rr-rr-rr-rr went the Grafanola.

And stopped.

For a moment all we could hear was the rain on the roof. The old man cleared his throat. "They're wearing out, these records," he said. "That's my problem. Play them too often, y'see. And the time's long gone when I could get another set. Which is where you two come in."

"Do we?"

"I want you to record them for me, all my records here... on tape, that is. Using one of those cassette things."

"Easy," I said. "Nothing high-tech about it, these days — provided you don't mind us recording all the scratches and crackles as well."

"Doesn't bother me a bit, son. By now the crackles and scratches are part of the song."

"Mister?" said Nimi. It was the first time she had spoken directly to him.

"Yes?"

"How will you play the tapes back?"

"What?"

Shy as ever, she shifted from one foot to the other. "If you want to play the tapes we make," she pointed out, You'll need a cassette-player of your own."

The old man nodded. "That's right."

"Can't you buy one?" I suggested. "Or maybe we could buy one for you as part of the Bob-a-Job."

He sat back in his chair, frowning. We could almost catch the sound of his brain weighing us up. "Would you do that for me?" he said at last.

"Sure."

"I'd be grateful, son."

"Er... we'd need some money, sir."

"Expenses, eh? Of course."

He reached for the walking-frame.

Probably it took only five minutes for him to cross to the chest of drawers covered by the dust-sheet, hitch up the cloth, stoop and pull open a drawer, but it felt like five hours.

Shuffling back to his chair with the brown paper envelope clamped under his arm and his bony hands prodding the frame ahead of him, he gasped for breath like a sprinter at the end of a race — except that, with a sprinter, you're not expecting it to sputter out any second.

"See... see how I'm trusting you?" he wheezed. "That's because you can always trust Boy Scouts. Got names, have you?"

"I'm Skip," I said.

"And I'm Nimi."

"Nimi? Sounds like a girl's name."

"It is, mister. Short for Nimisha."

"Nimisha?"

He blinked and screwed up his eyes. "You're not a Boy Scout, then?"

"A Girl Guide," I said quickly.

"That's fine. Just as good, they are. Here, Nimi, take this money. There should be enough there for one of these tape-player do-dabs. How soon can you get one?"

"Tomorrow, mister?"

"That would be wonderful. I'd appreciate it. If the home-help answers your knock next time, ask for me. The name's Archibald."

"Archibald?" I said.

"That's right. Like the song. One reason I'm so fond of it. What Archibald says goes... fair enough?"

43

"We'll do our best, Mr Archibald."

"Glad to hear it. Time for my rest now... you need lots of rests at my time of life. Give the door a hard bang as you leave, will you? Cheerio, Skip. And you, Nimi."

"Goodbye, sir."

"Bye, mister."

When we looked back across the room through all the piled-up furniture, he was still peering after us. Slowly he lifted a hand with three fingers upraised and the little finger tucked under his thumb. "The Boy Scout salute," I nudged Nimi.

We saluted back.

Going up the path we didn't say a word. At the main road, where dripping trees overhung the pavement, I halted. "Stuff it!" I said.

"What?"

"I forgot to give old Archibald his estimate for this Bob-a-Job. Taping all those records could take us ages. According to Dad, scouts could earn pounds and pounds for something really big. Reckon he'll pay us properly, Nimi?"

"Bound to."

I looked at her in surprise. "How come you're so certain?"

"This."

She offered me the envelope. All the way up the path she'd been counting the money, holding it under her anorak to keep it dry. "Check how much, Skip," she urged me. "I can't believe it."

Neither could I at first. I riffled through it again and again... then again, just to be sure.

It didn't take long.

After all, there were only twenty banknotes in the

envelope. But they added up to a nice, round, memorable figure. The money Mr Archibald had handed over for our expenses came to exactly a thousand pounds.

Chapter · Five

It was Nimi's job to buy the recorder and tapes, we decided. She knew the best cut-price shop in the neighbourhood near the factory where her mum worked. Also she had a secret place to hide all the cash that was left over — a place where she kept all her special things.

"What things?" I asked her.

"Just things."

"Are they valuable?"

"Not like this money, Skip. I've never seen so much money in my life. It takes Mum months to earn this amount even with all the extra shifts she can get and by the time she has we owe it all anyway. You will talk to your Dad about Mr Archibald, won't you?"

"I'll try."

"Or Ren, even."

"If I get the chance," I said.

Nimi looked at me anxiously. "Skip, you must. Suppose there are more envelopes like this in that drawer under the dust sheet... and suppose there's a break-in? Some burglar would cop the lot."

"What burglar's going to break in to a broken down dump like that, Nimi? And all the kids round here are scared stiff of the place."

"We weren't, Skip."

"Good point."

So the job I got lumbered with was asking advice about what we should do.

Ren would be my best bet, of course. Except Ren was the last person I wanted to talk to.

Anyway, talking to Dad would be a whole lot easier. He'd tell me off a bit about the Boy Scout fib, but he wouldn't really be upset. He'd be too interested in the whole situation. It was what he called *material*. That's the way authors are.

Once, when I was very little, Dad took me to a Book Fair where he was the guest-of-honour. People had come from miles around to hear him natter on about his writing and answer questions. Right at the end, a girl at the back of the hall stood up and said "Could I put a question to your son, please?"

Dad glanced down at me from the platform. "Can she, Skip?"

"Fine," I said.

The girl asked "What's it like to have a Dad who's an author?" I remember scratching my head about it. Then I said "I don't know... because I don't know what it's like to have a Dad who *isn't* an author."

Everyone thought this was brilliant. They clapped and clapped. Dad was still laughing about it as we drove home. It was a really smart answer, he reckoned.

The funny thing was, it was even smarter than he

realized. I was being tactful, you see. I knew for sure that the last thing the audience would want to hear is how Dad can be so wrapped up in his latest book, he's more like a zombie than a parent. The glamorous picture they had of writers would be wrecked forever.

That's why I wasn't keen on talking to him now.

Partly I was afraid he wouldn't pay proper attention because his mind would be on some imaginary adventure and partly I shrank from *too* much attention: he'd want me to spell out every detail from the way Mr Archibald moved — "like a scrawny statue, Dad, that's just come alive" — to the peculiar smell in the house — "Dad, it was all dampish and sour as if the whole place had wet itself."

I could just see him peering over his spectacles at me and sucking on the empty pipe he never lit these days but still refused to throw away. "Go on, Skip," he'd coax me.

Material, that's what he'd be after.

I did try to speak to him, though.

Honestly.

He was in his room, as usual, bent over his desk, when I stuck my head round the door. It had been a bad day, I could tell. There were bits of screwed-up paper all round his chair and his voice was tired and gritty. "That you, Skip?" he said over his shoulder.

"Dad..." I began.

"Here," he interrupted. "You've got a letter."

He held it up, his eyes still on his writing.

I recognized its thin, blue crispness straightaway: an airmail letter. From Mum, of course. To my annoyance, I saw it was addressed to Ren *and* me. We'd told Mum over and over again how much we hated having to share a letter between us and over and over again she'd promised to write us a letter each in future. Somehow she never did. Still, at least I was going to read this one ahead of Ren. Maybe that was the reason I forgot about Mr Archibald instantly.

The letter said:

Dear Skip and Ren,
How are you?
Is the move to the big city a success?
Even if it isn't, I'm pretty sure my favourite pair of kids in the Universe will be making the best of it, as usual. I bet you organized all the packing up between you while Dad was "just finishing the next chapter". Am I right? When I see you in October I'll be on the look-out for tell-tale signs of city-slickness so you'd better watch yourselves. Will you both be sporting bowler hats, I wonder, and snazzy briefcases? Or rapping out orders to all and sundry on one of those mobile phones?

If you haven't quite made it to tycoon status by the time I get back, though, don't worry. I quite like you the way you are, you'll be glad to hear. Knowing you, Skip, I reckon you'll be sussing the new scene for the rest of the holidays as if you've got your own next chapter to finish. And I expect Ren, in between propping up every lame duck she comes across, will be perfecting her Dead-Eye Dick routine with that dreadful catapult — okay, okay, I know we came to an agreement about it. Just be careful, that's all. A lethal object is still a lethal object however good-hearted the person holding it...

Ooops!

Am I doing my fusspot parent bit again? I can hear you grinding your teeth. I must admit it, I'm missing my family quite a lot these days. What with being covered in dust from bombed buildings, dodging snipers with itchy trigger fingers and trying to look like Ms Cool, star war correspondent, whenever a camera takes a sniff at me, I feel home is rather like a fairy-tale at present, even if it is by the Quaggy...

The QUAGGY for goodness' sake?

Personally, I think that husband of mine is barmy to swop the country for the city. Fancy leaving behind all that free fresh wind in his hair for no reason at all... though, come to think of it, he hasn't got much hair for the wind to be free and fresh IN, which may be the explanation. Tell the dear old Baldilocks I love him anyway even if he is stark, staring bonkers. And I love my two bears as well: Big Bear Ren and Little Bear Skip... Baldilocks and the two bears, geddit?

Must hurry now or the post will have gone. Write soon and so will I. Love you, love you both.

Kisses and cuddles from
Mummy Bear

She'd sent some photos, too — of herself and the camera crew sitting outside a restaurant, of a church-like building that was probably somewhere famous, of Mum shaking hands with a visiting rock star I recognized but couldn't name.

All in a day's work for her.

Or a day's play, rather. Mum was always careful to remind us her life abroad wasn't all muck and bullets. Also that she adored every minute of it.

I could hear her voice on the page as I re-read the letter — a voice very different from her clipped on-screen commentaries. Would it really be another three months before she burst through the front-door the way she always did, in an avalanche of luggage and jokiness, toting oddball presents from her latest faraway place and probably embarrassing us to death by dragging the taxi-driver behind her "to meet the best family ever and don't think I haven't checked my facts"? After hugs all round she'd say "bring me up to speed, team" and would listen for hours while we gave a blow-by-blow account of everything that had happened in her absence.

Our tough, gushy mum.

Mind you, I could just see Ren's face as she scanned this particular page. "Mummy Bear?" she'd sniff. "How old does she think we are? Mum spends so much time away she forgets we're not toddlers any more."

But she'd still take her turn to keep the letter, however feeble it was. Not to mention spinning a coin for first choice of the photographs. I glanced up to see if this was a good moment to show them to Dad.

He was hunched over his story, scribbling furiously, as if eager to make up for his duff day with a half-hour's brilliance before supper... a supper it was down to me to cook, obviously.

Yet again.

CHAPTER · SIX

The following day began badly. Mostly this was because I knew I'd let Nimi down. "Look," I sniffed. "It just wasn't *convenient* to talk to Dad."

Nimi didn't answer.

She'd barely uttered a word since we left home. Of course, she hardly needed to with her plastic bag saying it all. Packed inside was a small recorder, earphones, a lead already fitted with a plug and a half-dozen blank tapes, everything brand-new. Also it contained more than nine hundred pounds in cash: Mr Archibald's change. "I'll try again tonight," I promised.

"Skip, it's okay."

"Good."

It wasn't, though. She'd done her job, but I hadn't done mine. That was the truth of it. "The letter from Mum was what put me off," I went on. "She'll be coming home in the Autumn. You can meet her."

"Smashing," said Nimi.

"Ravi can meet her, too, if he's back from India." Nimi pulled a face. I looked at her curiously.

More than once I'd got the impression she wasn't too happy about Ravi's trip.

This didn't surprise me a bit. From what I'd heard, her big brother had been away for months and months, leaving Nimi to cope on her own with her tiny, widowed Mum. Still, this was none of my business as Ren would have pointed out. Nimi's silence was my business, though. Could she be *that* cross with me? Then I noticed the whiteness of her knuckles round the handle of the carrier-bag and the thin, tight line of her lips. At last the penny dropped. "Nimi, what's scaring you?"

"Nothing."

But her eyes were darting first to one side then the other as she took in every detail of the indoor market where we stood. It was supposed to be bolted and barred and kid-proof through the summer, but that didn't keep out, locals. It had seemed an obvious short cut to Mr Archibald's when we started out. "Shall we go back, Nimi?" I swallowed.

"Too late, Skip."

Too late for what?

Every square metre of the market felt like a threat now — from the glass-and-girder roof overhead to the open bays and lock-ups all round us. Even the cobbles beneath our feet couldn't be trusted. Wasn't it here the Quaggy went underground?

Quickly, I tried a favourite trick of mine. It's never failed me yet. What I do is conjure up in my mind every detail of the thing I'm afraid of. This means what actually happens is bound to be different because in real life things never turn out the way you predict. Everyone knows that.

So I imagined being ambushed right here by

Clint, Moxie, Olive and Johnny Chan.

I imagined them jeering at us, duffing us up, really mangling us. I even imagined two coffins—a Skip-sized one and a Nimi-sized one — being given a full Quaggy burial afterwards, opposite the sewer-pipe, with Mr Archibald's Grafanola blaring out music as they sank slowly to the riverbed.

Okay, so this was a bit of an exaggeration. Being an expert worryguts, I'd flipped through the whole scenario in less time than it took to reach the market's main courtyard. "Not much further, Skip," said Nimi with relief.

"Easy-peasy," I smiled.

We turned the corner into the stallholder's car park.

And stopped dead.

Straightaway I saw my imaginary script hadn't quite covered everything. The look on Clint's hard, handsome face, for instance. Lazily, he lifted a hand in greeting. " Hi, kiddiwinks," he said. " Nice of you to drop by."

The gang had pulled a couple of old trailers into an L-shape against the wall for somewhere to lounge, but the moment Clint shifted himself so did everyone else like courtiers who must never be better-placed than the king. Ren, too?

Ren, too.

Well, almost. Somehow she matched Clint move-by-move as if this court had an extra king. I saw the flicker in his eyes as he noticed it. "Look," I blurted out. "We're really sorry we've crashed in on you–"

"Sorry?" said Clint.

His smile was broader than ever. "Why be sorry, kiddiwink? Sorry's for softies. Be cool, instead. Like us."

"Yeah, like us," Moxie cackled.

"Cool," Clint said.

He glanced at Ren. "Got some plans for these kiddiwinks of yours, Renni-wenni?"

"Not a thing, Clinti-winti."

Moxie laughed and turned it, hastily, into a cough. Clint's smile now was about as friendly as a sharkbite. "Something amusing you, Mox?"

"Not a thing, Clint," Moxie said.

His face stiffened as he heard how close his words were to Ren's. "Just... just a tickle in the throat," he added.

"A tickle in the throat, huh?"

Clint touched his own throat with the lightest of fingertips. We saw Moxie shudder. Or did we all shudder? Apart from Ren, naturally.

She sauntered towards us. As usual, she seemed

to have all the time in the world. "Brought us a present?" she asked, reaching for Nimi's plastic bag.

I swear every rustle and clunk was deafening as she rummaged through it. She snorted with disgust. "Junk," she said. "Kiddiwink stuff."

"Is it?" drawled Clint. "Maybe I should take a look."

"Go ahead."

Ren held out the bag, trailing it from a finger. "All I'm saying is... it's kiddiwink stuff for *me*."

Clint's interest died at once. "Cool," he murmured.

He sprawled back against the trailer, idly tugging his rat's-tail. Again I saw the glint in his eyes.

Years ago, in a field near our house in the country, we had a mad horse. It had attacked its owner, we were told. He'd beaten it so often and so badly that one day it went berserk and kicked him practically into the next county. The trouble was, after this all the horse could do was kick people. "Dad, that's terrible,"I'd said. "I feel so sorry for it." I remember Dad nodding sadly. "So you should, Skip. It's damaged goods. Better make sure you feel sorry for it from a distance, though."

The reason this occured to me now was because Clint's eyes had a mad horse look.

Maybe he was mad.

Or maybe he'd copied the look from some film-clip as a useful tool to terrify. "Moxie?" he said suddenly.

"Yes, Clint?"

"Does the name William Tell mean anything to you?"

"William Tell?" Moxie said.

"A real cool dude, William Tell," said Clnt.

"Know what he did? I saw it on this video..."

"No?"

"It was cool. You see, he was a dead shot, this Tell dude. A double-top every time was about his mark."

"He was a darts-player, Clint?"

Clint sighed. "No, Moxie. This is history I'm talking about. He used to shoot this crossbow effort — smack where he was aiming at, no sweat. Know what his best trick was?"

"Sorry, Clint. Can't help you there."

"Moxie," said Clint heavily, "*I* know what his best trick was. I saw the video, right? I was only asking if *you* did. Want me to describe it to you?"

"Sure."

"You do?"

"Sure, Clint. That would be great."

"Moxie-poxie... you got lucky. You persuaded me. Well, this Tell bloke was once challenged to shoot an apple off his own son's head–"

As though an idea had just occurred to him, Clint broke off.

Except it was clearly part of his build-up.

When he spoke again, he tug-tug-tugged at his rat's-tail. "What a silly-billy I am... must be because I'm up to my armpits in kiddiwinks. Why should I *tell* the story? It was a video, right? *Watching* it is what we need."

Clint shaped his thumbs and index-fingers into a viewfinder, film-director style, peering through them as he swivelled in a long tracking shot from us to the wall opposite and back again.

Then, like a sound-man this time, he lifted a hand above his head and click-click-clicked to test the acoustic. In the shut-down market the snap of a cross-bow couldn't have been louder. "Ready to roll," he said. "Got an apple, Moxie?"

"An apple?"

"No apple, eh?"

Clint frowned. His eyes drifted to the plastic bag. "We'll just have to make do then, won't we... with kiddiwink stuff."

"Clint? You're not going to..."

"No, Moxie. I'm not going to eat the bag. The apple was for *aiming* at. A target, right? But the bag will be just as good. Easier to keep on the head for one thing."

He turned to Nimi and me. "Reckon you could balance that plastic bag?" he asked. "On both those bonces of yours? Up against that wall?"

He pointed. The wall was twenty or so metres away. "Of course," he went on, "it's Ren's choice whether she agrees to do it. Maybe she's not quite so good with her catapult as William Tell was with his crossbow..."

By now Moxie understood. Uneasily, he stared at his leader. "Er... you want her to hit that plastic bag from here, Clint? When it's balanced on these kids' heads over *there*? Suppose she misses the bag and hits them?"

"Yeah," Clint nodded. "Just suppose..."

"Is that all?" asked Ren.

"What?"

"Is that all you want me to do?"

"All?"

Clint's smile faded. "You got a better idea?"

"Just an improvement," said Ren. "Pro vided these two will go along with it. Will you?"

She was looking at me.

I remembered the petrol can in the grass and the flash of white across the Quaggy. Was this any different? "Why not?" I said.

"And you, Nimi?" Ren asked.

"Okay."

"Do exactly as I say, then."

"You'd better," said Clint.

So we did.

It's not much fun setting yourself up as a target. Soon Nimi and I had our backs against the brickwork, our arms round each other's waists and the weight of the bag on our heads as it slanted from me down to Nimi, held steady by the wall behind us.

"Don't flinch," Ren advised.

She didn't have to say why. In the pindrop silence of the market, her words were pebble-sharp, even at a distance of twenty metres.

"See the gap, Clint?"

"The gap?"

"Underneath the bag — surrounded by their faces and necks and shoulders. Where the brick shows through. It's bigger than an apple, I must admit. But there's more of them to hit if I miss."

"You're going for the gap?"

"Three shots," said Ren.

" *Three?*"

"To make sure it's not a fluke," said Ren. "That's what some of you thought last time, I seem to remember."

"Anything else?" said Clint, drily.

"Time me."

"What?"

"Time me. One of you with a watch. To see how

59

long I take — first shot to last shot."

"Got a watch, Moxie?"

"Sure, Clint."

"Time her, then."

Moxie unstrapped his watch and squinted at it in the palm of his hand. "Er... when from, Clint?"

"From whenever you give me the word," said Ren.

Already the catapult was in her left hand and stones were bunched in her right. She reminded me of a gunfighter at High Noon. Or a one-kid firing squad, maybe. Despite the muggy heat under the glass roof I was as icy all over as a fish on a slab. Nimi, too, so far as I could tell. At least our stillness would help Ren.

"Moxie?" Clint snapped. "You using a watch or a naffin' calendar?"

"Nearly ready, Clint."

I shut my eyes tight. A sound-track of what was coming would be quite vivid enough for me, thank you. I felt my pulse rate on overdrive, my heart pounding in my chest.

"Go!" shouted Moxie.

THWACK.

A puff of dust from the wall...

THWACK.

More dust and a tingling in my ear-lobe from a fragment of stone.

THWACK.

It was over. I coughed and opened my eyes. Nimi was coughing, too. She caught the bag as it fell into her arms. Midway between us, at about nose-height, a neat, tight triangle was chipped into the brickwork.

Nobody moved.

Ren had stone number four already in place and her catapult at full stretch though pointing nowhere in particular... except everyone knew who'd be first in line for it. "Remember this bit of the video, Clint?" she said gently. "The spare bolt William Tell kept handy in case he missed the apple and hit his son?"

"He didn't miss," said Clint.

"You got lucky, Clint. Neither did I."

"Six-and-a-half seconds," Moxie exclaimed. "All three shots in six-and-a-half seconds!"

"Not my best," Ren said.

"Isn't it?"

"I was being careful, Moxie. These are kiddiwinks, don't forget. Any big kid here want to take their place? I can do it much faster when I'm not so bothered about safety."

"Cool," said Clint.

Tug-tug-tug went his hand on his rat's-tail.

Slowly, not looking away from him, Ren slackened the catapult. "Skip?" she called. "Nimi? Get going. And make sure you don't come back. Next time I might lose my temper and shoot a hole through that kiddiwink bag of yours. Catch my drift?"

We didn't need to be told twice.

Outside, the air freshened us as we ran. Also, like pain that's worse when you relax, it brought on the jitters. The thwack of pebble into brick ricocheted on and on from one side of my brain to the other in time with the thud-thud-thud of our footsteps. We didn't slow down till we reached Mr Archibald's. There, under the trees where the track met the pavement, I had to own up. "Nimi?" I said thickly.

"Were you as scared of being hit as I was?"

"Petrified."

"Did you reckon she'd miss?"

"No... not Ren. She'd never take on something she couldn't do. What frightened me was the feeling I might panic and try to dodge and end up getting hit by accident. That's why I shut my eyes."

"So did I."

She looked at me gratefully. "Wasn't Ren brilliant, Skip? She fixed it so she saved us *and* kept secret what's in the bag. She's... she's unbelievable!"

"She is when she's toting that catapult. Did you see their expressions afterwards? They're convinced now she can practically pick their noses with it—thwack-thwack-thwack!"

"Outstanding..." Nimi murmured.

My sister was outstanding all right. By the skin of her teeth — or maybe I meant the skin of our faces — she'd even stuck to her rule about never aiming at a living target.

Miraculous, that was.

But how long could she keep it up?

CHAPTER · SEVEN

That morning, bit by bit, we learned more and more about Mr Archibald. "Scouts always were good listeners," he said.

"And Guides," I added.

"Guides too, yes."

We took it in turns to talk to him. While I made the recording in the furthest corner of the room, using furniture and dustsheets to baffle the sound, Nimi would keep the old man company over by the window.

Then we'd change places.

To begin with, anyway. Till we discovered that Nimi was much better at setting up the Grafanola and the tape-machine than I was, even if she did play safe by repeating everything twice over. Before deciding on the best place to record, she'd even checked out the back verandah overlooking the Quaggy. "Too draughty and delapidated," was her verdict.

Mr Archibald was enjoying himself. "Makes a change to have a really good chinwag," he said.

"Are you two having fun?"

"You bet," I said.

"Terrific," said Nimi.

Often Mr Archibald's voice would trail away altogether and his head sink onto his chest. But he never quite fell asleep. Just when I thought it was safe to tiptoe to the window and take my own peek at the Quaggy, he'd suddenly ask a question. "Skip," he said once, "do you know who this singer is?"

"Gracie Fields?"

"You've heard of her?"

"Her name's on the record."

"On millions of records, in actual fact. She was — what's the word for it these days? A superstar. Top of the bill at any theatre in the land, our Gracie. Made films, too. Over in Hollywood as well as here. Of course, her career had its ups-and-downs. Back in the war when she married this Italian bloke people said she'd gone over to the enemy. It would've finished most performers. She was soon forgiven, though. Ended up as a Dame."

"A Dame?" I said. "Like in pantomimes?"

"Not exactly, son. A Dame is a kind of Lady Knight. Being made one is a proper Buckingham Palace job. Arise, Dame Gracie — that sort of stuff. Would've been ' Sir Gracie' if she'd been a feller."

"Is she still alive, Mr Archibald?"

"Died in nineteen seventy-nine. Eighty-one years old. Younger than I am now. Funny that. Never thought I'd outlive Gracie Fields."

He was quiet for a while. Or maybe he was listening to Nimi, across the room, playing back the tape. Re-recording had muffled the song slightly but not enough to spoil it — not with all the crackles and hisses anyway. By this stage I knew every swoop and trill in that peculiar, needle-thin voice.

> *"I'm looking on the bright side*
> *Though I'm walking in the shade*
> *Flinging out my chest*
> *Hoping for the best*
> *Looking on the bright side of Life."*

It was dead granny-ish, I must say — and by that I mean both granny-ish *and* dead. Like all the others, this record belonged in a museum. It came from the days of steam trains and air-raid shelters and black-and-white newsreels so flickery you'd think it rained all the time. Dad mentioned those days sometimes. "Long gone," he always said. "Thank God."

It never seemed to cross his mind, or Mum's, that their Beatles songs sounded just as ancient to Ren and me.

> *"I'm waiting for the right tide*
> *And if luck comes to my aid,*
> *Giving me a break*
> *I shall be awake*
> *Looking on the bright side of Life."*

Mr Archibald coughed. "The wife's favourite song," he said. "Used to play it over and over again."

"When it first came out, sir?"

"Probably. Too long ago to remember now. The record belonged to her, though. So did the Grafanola, come to that."

"I thought you got it second-hand," I said.

"I did. From her after she died."

He fumbled for a cigarette. I frowned. He was the messiest smoker I've ever seen. "I know," he nodded. "Should've moved on to something more up-to-date, right?"

More up-to-date than cigarettes?

Drugs, did he mean?

Then I realized he was talking about the Grafanola. "Couldn't bear to trade it in after she'd gone, Skip. Kept it in working order for years and years, but never played it. Not till last summer, anyway. That's when I got it out again. Played it so often since then I'm surprised it's not worn itself out like the records. Brings the wife back to me, you see. She loved Gracie Fields. Used to copy the way she sang. Sounded just like her too. Sometimes, when I listen, I can't tell if it's Gracie or my old lady I can hear."

He lit the cigarette. Its tip glowed as he inhaled. He looked away from me, breathing out a stream of blue smoke that was fading already in the air around him. "Like a ghost you can switch on and off," he said.

He meant the Grafanola still.

At least, I think that's what he meant.

Then, like the cursor on a computer-screen, something in my brain blip-blip-blipped a connection. It had to be a connection. Wasn't it why we'd come in here in the first place?

I took a deep breath. If I didn't speak soon I'd lose my nerve and the chance would be lost. "Since *last summer*?" I said.

"What?"

Mr Archibald bent forward, his eyes straining to get me into focus. That's when I knew I was right. "Last summer, Mr Archibald?" I repeated. "Isn't that what you said?"

"You remember what happened last summer, Skip?"

"The kid," I said.

"You do, then."

"He drowned, didn't he? Over by the sewer-pipe? There was a special assembly about it at school, Nimi says. But that was before I moved here. All I know is he was some local boy."

"So I heard... I heard."

A dollop of ash fell on his cardigan.

I'm not surprised with his hand trembling so much. His voice was trembly, too — if a husky whisper can be trembly. "It was the worst day of my life," Mr Archibald went on. "Even losing the wife, wasn't as bad in some ways. At least that was natural — terrible but natural. Listening to a youngster drown, though... knowing you can't get there in time or even see him properly if you did, let alone save him... it turned my stomach. Made me throw up, I don't mind telling you. Of course, I 'phoned for help straight-away — but I always knew it was too late, Skip. All the splashes and shouting... on his own, he was. Died on his own."

I said nothing.

Behind the dustsheets and furniture, Nimi had somehow picked up what we were talking about. Without fuss, in her tactful Nimi-like way, she'd stopped the machines.

The sound of her *not* recording nearly deafened me.

Hardly aware of doing it — like Dad fiddling with his pipe —Mr Archibald lit another cigarette. "Stupid..." he said. "Just plain stupid to let it get to me. Happens all the time these days, I dare say —

people killed on the roads and suchlike. Saw a lot of good mates snuff it in the war, too... lots of them. Wasn't the same, though. This just wasn't the same. So *unnecessary*."

"Did it happen just after you moved in?"

"What?"

"It stopped you unpacking, didn't it?"

"Unpacking?"

"All these dust sheets and tea chests," I said patiently. "Even Dad got everything sorted out eventually once we'd moved in. And we had about a million books to unload."

Mr Archibald shook his head. "You've got the wrong end of the stick, Skip. This stuff isn't for unloading — it's ready to go. I'll be leaving here pretty soon. Need a bit of looking after now, you see. Started bumping into things, falling over. The home-help can't cope any more, bless her."

"Where are you off to?"

"Nowher e special. Doesn't have to be special when you're as long in the tooth as I am. Just a nursing home by the sea. I like the sea. Always happy living near water. Till last summer, anyway. And the sea's nothing like the Quaggy."

He glanced towards the window.

Outside, the clouds were breaking up, bringing sunlight and patches of blue. Also green-ness instead of the dreary paving-stone grey that summed up the city for me. From here you'd hardly know there was a city out there at all.

Or a drowning.

Mr Archibald sighed. "So I've sold up, Skip. All signed and sealed, it is. Got rid of everything — or soon will have. My nest-egg is over there in the bottom drawer. More than enough to see me through. Don't trust banks, y'see. Can't abide 'em. Along with a few personal knick-knacks that's all I'll be taking with me."

"Not even the Grafanola?" I asked.

"Don't need it now, do I? Nor those clumsy old records. They're redundant thanks to you two. A good job, you're doing. That little machine you've bought will suit me fine. Especially with earphones. Less anti-social."

He chuckled as he stubbed out his cigarette. "Gracie Fields' fans are a bit thin on the ground these days," he said.

"Er... Mr Archibald?"

"Son?"

"That money you gave us. It was much too much for what we bought. We've brought back over nine-hundred pounds."

"That so?"

He didn't seem very interested. "Put it with the rest, will you? Save me getting up. Getting up's a bit of a chore for me to tell the truth."

"No problem."

We'd left the plastic bag by Mr Archibald's chair. I took out the wad of notes and crossed to the chest of drawers under the dust sheet. The bottom one slid open quite easily — to my surprise when I saw how full it was. It was crammed almost to the top with bundles like the one I'd got in my hand, pile after pile after pile of them. "Mr Archibald?" I yelped.

No answer.

This time he really was asleep, snoring gently.

I gaped down at the drawer. Of course, without unpacking it, I couldn't be sure how deep the money went, how many levels there were below the one I could see.

But Mr Archibald certainly didn't trust banks.

There was enough money here to buy a Rolls Royce to take him to his new home by the sea... chauffeur-driven. In fact, Mr Archibald could have afforded just about anything that took his fancy for the rest of his life. My voice, when I finally got it back, came out as a croak. "Nimi?"

"Skip?"

"What do you think of this?"

Being a kid who had to count every penny she ever got, she was gobsmacked the instant she looked over my shoulder. Or I think she was. She turned away too quickly for me to be certain — her eyes on the old man in the wicker chair dozing in the Quaggy sunshine.

"Should've guessed, I suppose," she said. "It was pretty obvious what we'd find."

Then she managed a laugh. "Lucky for him you're a Boy Scout, Skip. And I'm a Girl Guide."

CHAPTER · EIGHT

We needed to think.

So we told Mr Archibald we hadn't quite finished the recordings and would be back later in the week for one last session. "Fine," he said. "Drop in whenever it's convenient. You're always welcome here."

"He meant it, too," I said as we left. "He was smiling so much I thought his false teeth were going to fall in his lap."

"He likes us being there, Skip."

"He likes visitors — any visitors. Gives him the chance to natter, poor old bloke."

"Rich old bloke," said Nimi. "I've never seen such a stack of money in my life."

"Me neither."

"Haven't you?"

"Nowhere near."

"Really?"

I sighed and tried to explain. "Writers, even quite well-known ones like Dad, aren't terrifically well-paid, Nimi. And my mum runs her own production company — which she's still setting up so she's had to

71

borrow thousands. She may be mega-wealthy one day, she says, but not for a long while yet."

"Oh," Nimi said.

I could tell she didn't believe me. No one ever did, especially round here. Ren reckoned they were right. "Compared with most kids we are rich," she said. "Think about it, Skip. What Mum and Dad haven't got is mostly what they can't be bothered with anyway. Doesn't that count as rich?"

Okay, she had a point. It didn't help me deal with Mr Archibald's dosh, though. Even talking about it frightened me.

I wasn't the only one. Nimi was actually shaking. "Let's go to my hideout," she pleaded. "We'll be safe there."

"Your hideout?"

"Where my special things are. I told you, Skip. But you must promise never to reveal–"

"Sure," I interrupted.

Did she think I didn't know about hideouts?

Well, I didn't.

Not this kind.

For a start, the electricity sub-station was a put-off. As we slid along the gap between its wire fence and the motorway, it was hard to decide if the gentle hum we could hear was high voltage or traffic-vibration.

Next, we crossed a concrete causeway with a sort of paved ditch on either side. "What is it?" I asked. "Drainage?"

"The Quaggy."

"Yeah?"

We took a sharp turn to the left under a huge stone-clad pillar, one of a dozen supporting the fly-

over above, and arrived at last at a bank of sand and gravel where someone had hollowed out a kind of foxhole.

Nimi, was it?

She nodded. "Last year, Skip. I used to come here a lot."

"Bit pongy, isn't it?"

"From the rats, probably."

"Rats?"

"They won't show up while we're around."

"Choosy, huh?"

She smiled. "Neither will anyone else, though. That's why I made this my den. At least it's private even if it is a bit plain."

Putrid is the word I'd have used.

More-or-less under the bank's overhang, I scooped out a seat in the shingle. "Where's your things?" I asked. "I thought this was where you kept them?"

"Close by, Skip. In a tin box that locks."

"Buried?"

"In the gravel."

"Neat."

Where the rats couldn't nibble it. And where yobs or winos wouldn't think to look. Compared with my stamping ground in the country, this was a different universe. For instance, were those skimpy objects on top of the bank supposed to be trees? More like leafy, overgrown antennae. As the breeze caught them, the pattern of shadows they sent skittering across the face of the flyover made me feel queasy in the stomach. "It's a bewilderness..." I said.

"What?"

"Mum's phrase."

"I know."

She lifted a hand to keep me where I was.

A moment later, from beyond the bank, I heard gravel being shifted and the clink of a key in a lock. When she returned she was carrying a small radio-recorder. "It's Ravi's," she said. "I'm taking care of it while he's away."

"Will he mind?"

"Of course not. Probably the batteries are a bit flat, though. It may not be very good."

Considering she'd taped it from television, it was brilliant. I heard Mum's voice clear as clear:

"... not a pretty sight. Here violence, and the effects of violence, are a matter of routine. The victims have suffered so much, they can't afford to care any more. And it's an open question whether those responsible ever cared in the first place..."

"She's ace," Nimi beamed.

"The best," I said. "Why did you tape-record it, though?"

"I've been taping her programmes since I first found out she was your mum, Skip. I've never known anyone famous before. Well, I almost know her."

That wasn't what I'd meant. "Um... Dad puts them all on video," I said. "Every one of them. Shall I play a few tapes back to you sometime?"

"Would you?"

"Sure."

"Skip, that would be brilliant. Mum and me will be getting a video soon, I reckon."

When Ravi got back?

No, I didn't actually say this. I wasn't that gross. Instead, I brought up the subject we'd been avoiding. "About Mr Archibald, Nimi..."

"Yes?"

"This money of his, rather..."

"What about it, Skip?"

She looked at me expectantly. I wasn't sure how to go on. What could I say to persuade her that this was *our* adventure, and it was down to us to see it through? Even Ren wouldn't have turned up her nose at what we'd got into.

So tough luck, Ren. Big sister had missed out on the action, for once.

Or Big Brother?

I stared at Nimi. How could I have been so dim? It wasn't just me—*she* had some paying back to do as well. Why hadn't I spotted this before? "You want us to sort it out by ourselves as much as I do!" I accused her. "Because of Ravi."

"Ravi?"

"Ravi, yes. Off on his famous trip abroad. Serve him right if he misses this that's how you feel, am I right?"

"Think so?"

"Nimi, I know so. So why not admit it?"

I'd never seen her so uncomfortable.

"Okay, Skip. I admit it," she said. "Now tell me what we *do*."

"Bring the money here," I said.

"What?"

"It's obvious, Nimi."

I sat back. I suppose I was as cool as I'd ever been in my life. "People break into houses all the time, don't they? Ever heard of anyone breaking into a waste-tip? It doesn't make sense. So this is just the spot to hide the banknotes till Mr Archibald leaves for the seaside. Is that tin box of yours big enough?"

"It's more like a trunk, Skip. Almost empty."

"Perfect."

"But how do we get the money here?"

"That's the tricky bit. We'll have to keep our eyes skinned every step of the way. Just like we did this afternoon. Maybe we could disguise it somehow or move it after dark. Could you get to this place after dark?

"Skip, I've done it."

"No problem, then."

Just details, that's all. We could work out a few details couldn't we?

Carefully, we stashed away the recorder and covered out tracks in the gravel. As we slipped back under the flyover, re-crossed the causeway and eased ourselves side-by-side past the sub-station—all as if we were no more than a couple of kids on the mooch — my brain buzzed with the biggest Bob-a-Job ever. For the first time since Dad had moved us to the city I felt in charge again.

In charge, that's right.

Maybe that's why it came as such a shock when Nimi and I turned the corner of our street and saw the pair of them—Dad and Ren—sitting side by side on our front steps, waiting for us.

Instantly, I knew.

I knew it from the way they stood up, white-faced, as we approached and from the sudden chill in my stomach as if I'd been struck by a bolt of ice.

"It's Mum, isn't it?" I said.

"Skip..."

"Isn't it?"

Dad tried to speak but the words wouldn't come. Not that I needed them. I'd dreaded this moment, and rehearsed it, all my life. "How is she, Dad?" I heard myself say. "Is it bad?"

I saw Ren take Dad's hand.

As I looked up the steps towards them, they went blurry in my vision and every daft detail behind their heads came into such sharp focus it was printed on my memory forever: our stone porch and the brickwork behind it; the crooked line of our gutter; the shape of our chimneypots against a drift of clouds.

In real life, as everyone knows, things never turn out the way you predict. But you can't change what's already happened.

I tried, though. Even then I really, really tried. "Dad?" I begged. "Aren't you still holding your breath for her... just a little bit?"

He blinked, not understanding. Then he remembered our family motto and almost smiled before his eyes filled with tears. As he held out his arms to cuddle me, or maybe to get me to cuddle him, I noticed Ren was crying too.

Ren?

That's when I knew for sure how bad it was.

CHAPTER · NINE

Mum was killed by a complete accident.

It wasn't a bomb or a bullet or a collapsing building that finished her off the way we'd expected. Being a star war-correspondent had nothing to do with it. Instead, off-duty, she'd been crushed by a tour-bus which swerved out of control and ploughed through the roadside café where she was the only person having a meal. A silly end, really, for someone like her.

But she was still gone.

We couldn't ask for a script-change on the grounds that her ending wasn't grand enough.

Even so, she got a hero's send-off from just about the whole country. Every news-bulletin mentioned her, every headline screamed her name. Our house, which was pretty untidy to start with, got cluttered up still more by an avalanche of letters and cables and flowers. For a while we were up to our ears in reporters all thrusting cameras and microphones at us. Then, after the memorial service, interest faded away. Mum was yesterday's item.

At first I was angry about this till it dawned on me how Mum would have reacted. "News is like that," she'd have said. "What do you want it to be — *olds*?"

Ren smiled when I mentioned it. "That's Mum all over," she agreed.

"*Was* Mum" I said.

"Okay, *was* Mum. And we're us, Skip. We've got to put this behind us, right? For Dad's sake... and ours."

Dad was brilliant, I must admit. When we wanted to grizzle he let us grizzle, when we wanted to talk he let us talk. "Gives me the chance to do a bit of grizzling and talking as well," he said.

He even watched some of Mum's tapes with us and helped us make a scrapbook of her letters and postcards from all over the world. We also spent ages writing back to everyone who'd written to us, often sounding much more serious on paper then we did across the table from each other. "Occupational therapy," Dad called it.

His own occupational therapy began about a week afterwards. As I lay in bed on a gusty, moonlit night, I heard the tap-tap-tap of his word-processor upstairs. I slipped into Ren's room to tell her.

"He's turning Mum into material," I said.

"Not yet," said Ren. " It doesn't happen that soon. But he will eventually, I guess."

"How will we feel when we read about it?"

"Better than we do now, Skip."

"You reckon?"

I wasn't so sure.

To tell the truth, I couldn't work out what my feelings were. It wasn't as if Mum had left a gap the way most mums would. How could we miss someone we'd never got used to having around in the first place?

For us it was more like an official announcement that birthdays had been abolished or Christmas no longer existed. Simply, the best of all our treats had gone forever. We had to *remind* ourselves there'd be no more shared letters to grumble about, no more crazy presents to unwrap, no more sessions where we just sat around bringing each other up to speed. I turned away hastily in case I started to blub again. "Night, Sis," I choked.

On my way back to bed, it would have been easy to fool myself that nothing much had really altered. Certainly the view from our landing window was no different: the same flicker of cars on Vandyke Hill, the same blink of shop-signs in the precinct. Bundled up in my dressing-gown, torn between the sleep I needed and the hug I wanted from Dad, I could almost believe the tremble of floorboards under my feet was caused by the same passing train I remembered from a fortnight before.

Except Mum had been alive then.

And no rain whispered in the Quaggy tonight. If I hadn't known it was there, my mind would have shied away from the very idea of it.

A river?

In a place as built-up as this?

I'd be telling myself next about slopes so over-grown they almost hid a rickety old house overlooking water so deep and weed-choked it could drown you. What's that? There's treasure in the house, too —a bottom-drawer stuffed with bank notes?

Get away!

Of course, if this were a story I'd simply invent the

ending I fancied — making sure it was a lot better than true. Real life was a bit more complicated. "Too complicated for me," I said out loud.

"Skip?" said Ren.

I jumped, startled.

My sister had followed me onto the landing. I could see her reflection in the window alongside mine, lit from behind by the giant moon of her bedside lamp, so we looked like a pair of huge, phantom sleepwalkers hovering over the Quaggy. "Just... just talking to myself, Ren," I said.

"Really?"

She grinned at me in the glass. I grinned back, sheepishly. "The first sign of madness," I said.

"Only if you give yourself an answer, Skip."

"Ren, I wish I could. I'm not even sure what the questions are. All I know is... is..."

"It's not finished," she said. "That's what you know."

"Isn't it?"

"Not according to Nimi."

"Nimi?"

"I've been talking to her, Little Bruv. She's okay, Nimi. Been a big help to me these last few days. You've picked a good friend there."

"You bet," I said.

Actually, I hadn't given Nimi a thought for ages. It was typical of Ren to make it sound as though I'd been making space for the two of them to get acquainted. "What did she say?" I asked.

"Not much. But all of it made sense."

"Tell me."

"She'll tell you herself."

"Nimi will?"

Ren was staring past my reflection now out into a city darkness which clearly scared her no more than city brightness did. Even as I watched, a car turned onto Vandyke Hill so its headlights seemed to flash from my sister's eyes a moment before gliding up, up into the night. "Skip," she said. "Nimi reckons it's time you got it sorted out — this business at the old house near the bend in the Quaggy. No, she didn't spell out the details. Apparently she left a note there this morning, though. To say she'll be paying a visit first thing tomorrow."

"Tomorrow?"

"Tomorrow, Skip. She wants you to meet her. I told her I thought you'd be able to handle it. Was that okay?"

"Tomorrow?" I said again.

"Why not, Skip? Unless you prefer Nimi to tackle it on her own. And she will, you know. She's tougher than you think. Is that what you want?"

"No," I said.

"So you'll go?"

I shrugged. "Why not?"

After all, would our madcap Mum have left things dangling? Probably Mr Archibald was the only person in the country who hadn't heard of her.

Strangely, that was a help.

CHAPTER · TEN

Next day, would you believe, I overslept. Nimi was already on the verandah, banging the knocker, when I arrived. The door opened so promptly Mr Archibald must have been waiting behind it with his hand on the latch. His eyes lit up when he saw us. "You'll be chuffed to bits you've come," he said.

"Will we?"

"Got a surprise for you both. Shouldn't wonder if there wasn't an extra badge in it for the pair of you!"

Why was he so pleased with himself?

As he led us across to the window at the usual walking-frame pace, every step he took brought another snorting giggle. "What's so funny?" I asked.

"Funny, son?"

Something was. Mr Archibald was still grinning as he eased himself into his chair.

For a moment he just sat there, blinking. We'd seen this before. Maybe he was so old now he had to re-stock with energy the instant he used some up.

I looked around me.

Why did it feel so different? Everything was just

the same, wasn't it — apart, that is, from today's dazzling sunshine? This spilled through the room bringing a gentle glow even to the darkest, most spidery corner. For the first time I saw smudges by the front door where pictures had hung — pictures packed up under the dustsheets, I supposed. Had the dustsheets themselves been shifted?

No, they were exactly in place.

Mr Archibald got his breath back. We heard his teeth click as he cleared his throat. "I've done you a favour, Skip," he said. "You and Nimi."

"Have you?"

"You deserve it, mind. Both of you. Beyond praise how you've tackled this recording project — so careful and efficient. Polite, too. And cheerful. That's what I appreciate most, probably. How you've cheered me up. So I've said so."

"Said so?"

"To your patrol leader."

"Our..."

My mouth went dry. "Our patrol leader, Mr Archibald?" I said. " In the Scouts, you mean?"

"And the Guides. Didn't know they'd merged, to tell the truth. Seems peculiar to me — boys and girls in the same troop. Not the way it was in my day. Handy, though. Can't deny that. Meant I was able to put in the same good word for each of you. Might've got you promoted, I shouldn't wonder. Would you like that? To win another stripe, or another star, whatever it is?"

"Smashing," I said.

He frowned, disappointed. "Have I done something wrong? Embarrassed you, have I?"

"No," I said quickly. "An extra badge would be

terrific. Really ace. I'm just puzzled how... how you managed to get in touch with our patrol leader, that's all."

"Ah, so that's it! You've been caught on the hop. Sorry about that — but it's what a spot check is *for*, after all."

"A spot check?" said Nimi. "On us?"

"Nothing to worry about, my dear. He's thrilled, your patrol leader. Really thrilled. The whole patrol is. Reckoned it was the best Bob-a-Job he's come across in a long time — in fact, he wants to congratulate you, personally.

"Fine," I said. "We'll... we'll call in at the Scout Hut on our way home."

"No need," Mr Archibald smiled.

"What?"

"That's my surprise, Skip! I told them you'd be popping in this morning to put a few finishing touches to the tapes. So you'll get your pat on the back right here."

"This morning?" I said. "The patrol leader is coming here this morning?"

"Better than that, son."

He was beaming with pleasure. Suddenly, at the top of his weirdly deep voice he called out "DYB! DYB! DYB! Do Your Best!"

The answer, from behind the furniture-stacks, rang up into the rafters. "DOB! DOB! DOB! We'll Do Our Best!"

Slowly, Nimi and I turned round.

Each of them held a hand upraised in a three-fingered salute as they stepped into the sunlight. So did their patrol leader, except he used his to tug-tug-tug at his rat's-tail haircut. "Greetings, Skip," he said.

"Greetings, Nimi."

"Hello, Clint."

"Did you say something?"

"Hello Clint," we repeated, louder.

"That's better. Let's have a bit of enthusiasm round here—a bit of keenness, eh?"

Moxie and the others had shuffled into line. They stood to straggly attention, heads up, shoulders back, arms flat to their sides. "Pity your sister's not here," Clint said. "Pleased as punch, she'd be."

"Isn't she with you?" I asked.

"Ren?"

He tried to remember. "Maybe she's back at Headquarters," he said. "Having her woggle turned up."

"Your sister?" said Mr Archibald. "You've a sister, Skip?"

"You bet," said Clint. "He's got a sister all right...

take it from me. But she won't be along today, I'm afraid. Shame that. Things won't be the same without her."

"Why not give her a full-report later on, son?"

"Good idea, Mr Archibald."

Clint gave a crisp salute. Delighted, Mr Archibald saluted back. He was sitting bolt upright in his chair, elbows tucked in, feet close together, like a V.I.P. at a parade.

Already Clint was deep into some Oscar-winning performance as a sergeant-major. He strutted along the row, tweaking Olive's sleeve into place here, flicking away a speck of dust from Johnny Chan's collar there. Moxie's turn took longest. Clint shook his head wearily. " Naff," he said. " Totally naff. Those shoe-laces just aren't regulation, kid. The wrong knots for a start — granny knots, aren't they? Didn't I tell you they should be *reef* knots? Right over left and left over right?"

"Sorry, Clint. I forgot."

"Forgot. You *forgot*?"

"Slipped my mind, Clint."

"Yeah? A slip-knot, eh? Sort it out, kid, or I may be forced to tie a sheepshank with your windpipe. And while you're at it, kindly shine up those boots of yours. They're a disgrace."

"My boots, Clint?"

"By tomorrow I want them glittering — positively glittering. Got it? So I can see my own smile staring back at me from your toecaps."

Moxie was horrified. "These are Doc Martens, Clint!"

"So?"

"But no one ever shines..."

"Yes?"

"...okay, Clint."

"Glad that's settled. Anything else?"

"No, Clint."

"Good."

Mr Archibald bent forward, lowering his voice to a whisper everyone in the room could hear. "Skip, he's good this patrol leader of yours. Knows what he wants. Keeps up standards. Did I tell you how he found out you were here? One of the patrol saw Nimi give me a salute yesterday when she handed over the note. So he decided on this spot-check today. Smart management, that. No cause for you to fret, though. I've told him everything."

Everything?

Not everything, obviously. If they'd known that much, his visitors would have left already with bulging pockets and fatcat grins.

The inspection was over. Legs apart and hands behind his back to show them how, Clint rapped "Stand easy!"

"Bravo!" Mr Archibald applauded.

"Thanks, Guv," said Clint. " Might I have a word with young Skip, here? A private word if that's in order. Scout-business, you understand..."

"Go ahead, son. Why not step out onto the verandah behind us? You'll find the key in the lock, I think. Better watch where you're treading, though— some of the planks out there are a touch rotten. But it's definitely private. If you pull the door shut we won't hear a thing."

"Much obliged, Mr Archibald. I'll leave the troop in your good hands if I may."

"Me?"

"Every one of them is still on duty, mind. So don't let them move a muscle. Not a muscle, Guv. Okay?"

"My pleasure, son."

Clint jerked a thumb for me to follow him.

Desperately, I tried to catch Nimi's attention as I passed but she was still staring ahead of her, too fazed even to notice.

Out on the verandah, Clint began by checking the woodwork. A *touch* rotten, was it? More like crumbling with rotten-ness. A couple of heavy jumps from either of us and the whole flimsy structure — floorboards, railings, uprights and roof — would have collapsed at once into the water. Scarier still, it seemed to be held up at one end by nothing more than an old, tightly-coiled rope fastened high under the eaves.

Clint eased the door shut behind him. As he scanned the bend in the river, his gaze lingered on the sewer pipe. " A kid drowned here once," he said. "Know that, did you?"

"Yes."

"Over there, it was. Last Summer. Caused quite a kerfuffle in these parts — it being so close to the main road an' all. That's why kids won't come here any more."

"Don't they?"

"Mostly, they don't. Too scared, you see, because of the accident... if it was an accident."

"Wasn't it, then?"

"Who can say, Skip? Except the drowned kid, of course. Not much chance of an answer there."

"Suppose not."

"Anything could've happened."

"Suppose so."

"Do you?"

90

Clint was fiddling with his rat's tail again: tug-tug-tug. "I like a kid who can suppose," he said. "Shows imagination. Important, that. A kid with imagination can go far. So let's suppose a bit more, you and me. Okay?"

"Okay."

"You can start, Skip. For instance, suppose you tell me about Ren."

"Ren?"

"Your sister, yes. That Ren. Suppose you let me in on why a classy kid like her would take up with a bunch of tearaways like us."

"Why shouldn't she?"

"Why shouldn't she? Because you're not like us, Skip. You're like *you*. Haven't you noticed? No, don't shrug... *suppose*. I mean, what if she's some kind of spy for the Juvenile Bureau? An infiltrator, say. Yeah, there's the word. An *infiltrator*."

"That's stupid."

"Is it?"

"Ren's not sneaky. She doesn't have to be."

"Right," said Clint. "Not with that catapult of hers." He nodded, thoughtfully.

Below him, the weed-green Quaggy slapped at the house's foundations. Clint's gaze probed it for an answer. This close, and without his bodyguards to pad him out, his height and weight were almost normal though not to the point where you fancied your chances. Every move he made was electric with menace.

He lifted a finger. "Suppose..." he went on.

"Yes?"

"Suppose... she was sussing me out for one of your Dad's books? Yes, Skip — I've heard all about

91

your Dad. Could we be... you know... what's the word for the stuff a writer writes about?"

"Material," I said.

"Material , that's it. Don't fancy being *material* much. Is that what Ren's after? A bit of rough to fill up a chapter? Or maybe for one of your mum's television programmes... oops! Sorry, Skip. I was forgetting your mum won't be making any more television programmes. Shouldn't have mentioned that, should I?"

"Please yourself," I said.

He paused to check on the impact he'd made. I stared back, expressionlessly. He frowned. "So what *is* Ren up to Skip?"

"Maybe she just likes you, Clint."

"What?"

My words hadn't come out right. The lump in my throat had blunted the sarcasm. But I didn't want to say it again. Not with his eyes eating me up. "What?" he repeated.

We stood there in one of those silences you can hear ticking like a bomb.

At our feet, the Quaggy slid on regardless.

Eventually, Clint sniffed and shifted his position. His eyes had gone hard again. "Okay, Skip. Let's do some different supposing. Like, suppose you explain this Bob-a-Job business? Why are you faffing around with an old geezer on the brink of snuffing it? Doesn't add up, that."

"He told you, Clint. We're putting all Mr Archibald's records on cassette before they wear out. Somehow we just got involved with the Scout and Bob-a-Job thing — and now it's too late to put it right. It was just an accident."

"Oh, an accident," Clint nodded. "Like the drowning."

I'd heard this before about Clint — how he twisted your words till you were too flustered and terrified to argue.

After this, kids said, came the knife.

The knife, yes.

It was in his hand now — a claspknife with a chunky handle and a blade so sharp and so stubby it looked like an overweight razor. Idly, he tilted it this way and that making it flash in the sun. "This is my Little Friend, Skip," he said. "Ever met my Little Friend?"

"No."

"Dearie me. Still, not to worry. My Little Friend is dead easy to get on with. Provided you do like she says, that is. If you don't she can get distinctly... snippy. Definitely *snippy*. Understand?"

"Yes."

"Thought you would. So let's re-run that last bit shall we? Because I don't think I've got the full strength of it yet. And that makes me nervous..."

He lifted the knife.

From the far side of the house we heard a door slam.

The front door?

Almost before the sound had died away, Clint's blade had vanished. He snatched at my arm, twisted it into a savage half-Nelson and bundled me back in the house with a sudden shove that sent me sprawling across the floor. When I looked up, I saw nothing in the room had changed... well, not much. Stretched out against his cushions, Mr Archibald had drifted off into one of his naps. Clint's gang, though, was wide-awake with fright as they stared at the space where

93

Nimi had been. "She's gone?" Clint hissed.

"Er... she just walked out on us, Clint," said Moxie.

"You didn't stop her?"

"How could we? We're on parade — not allowed to move a muscle. That's what you said, Clint."

I laughed out loud, hoping to rouse Mr Archibald. He didn't even stir. "Cool," said Clint.

But no cooler than he was.

He wasn't acting now.

Watching him *not* lose his temper was more chilling than any tantrum would have been. His eyes slid from Moxie to me to Mr Archibald. "Did she say anything before she left?" he asked.

"Only..."

"Yes?"

Moxie flicked a glance at me. Clint nodded, getting the message. "Skip," he murmured, "kindly wait for us out on the verandah, will you? This is confidential."

"But Clint–" I protested.

"*Do* it," he said.

CHAPTER · ELEVEN

Would Ren try to rescue me?

No question — assuming Nimi found her. But how long would that take? And what could my sister do once she'd arrived? I mean, out here with the Quaggy between us? I felt dizzy with panic.

To my left, midway between the jut of the verandah and the slope of the bank, a tiny island of earth like a marooned burial mound was all that broke the river's sour, polluted surface. Was it close enough to be reached in one flying leap... followed by another onto dry-ish land? Easy enough, I decided. Provided you had wings attached to your ankles.

Ren was my only hope.

But she'd better be quick. Already I heard a shuffle of footsteps and the scrape of the back door as the Clint and Co. Scout Troop filed out onto the verandah.

Moxie came first, testing his weight on the floorboards ahead of him. He was carrying a pile of records. So were each of the others. It looked like Mr Archibald's entire collection. "What are you doing with those?" I asked.

"Guess," said Clint.

He lounged against the handrail opposite. Beneath my feet, I felt a tremor of woodwork like the shift of a ship at anchor. Clint glanced up at the rope under the eaves. "See that?" he said. "Doesn't look much, does it? Take it from me, though, that rope's all there is between us and a plunge in the gunge. So be cool, team. Be really cool."

"Reckon it's safe, Clint?" Moxie asked.

"It's perfect."

Clint meant the whole situation — his nerve against everyone else's.

Slowly, his gaze wandered over us till it got as far as me. "Skip?" he said.

"Yes?"

"Tell me again why you're here."

"You know why."

"Taping these records, was it?"

I nodded eagerly. "They belonged to Mr Archibald's wife. She was a fan of this famous old singer called Gracie Fields. Played her songs over and over again, he says. So every time he listens to them he's reminded of her. According to him, it's *her* voice he hears — his wife's I mean. They're like a... like a memento."

"That so? This record, for instance?"

Clint took one from Moxie, twirling it between the flats of his hands in its brown paper sleeve. "Great title," he said. "Cop this team — sorry, patrol, I should say. It's called ' What Archibald Says Goes'. Neat, that — being his name an' all. Fond of this one, is he?"

"One of his favourites," I said.

"Oh, a *favourite*. Well, I never. So he'd be espe-

96

cially sorry to lose it, then. Eh, Skip?"

"Yes."

"I thought as much."

Casually, like a kid tossing a frisbee, Clint sent the record spinning up, out, over the Quaggy.

It hovered a moment just short of the sewer pipe, flipped itself vertical, and vanished underwater with scarcely a splash.

Clint tapped his nose, thoughtfully. "Mr Archibald was right," he said. "That one certainly went — maybe because of the weight. Dead solid these old seventy-eights. Reckon this one will go as well? Should do, judging by the title. 'Wish Me Luck As You Wave Me Goodbye'. Sounds promising to me. Goodbye, record... and good luck."

"Don't," I said.

"Don't? Decided to talk, have you?"

"There's nothing more to say."

"No?"

Again came a flick of the wrist, a whirl of brown paper and a slicing, edge-on dive into the water.

Taking his time, Clint chose another. "'A Little Lake in London'!" he exclaimed. "What a coincidence! Must mean the Quaggy, here. Well... as near as makes no odds."

This one bounced twice on the surface, ducks and drakes style, before it vanished.

That's how it went on.

And on.

Next came "Sally" and "Little Old Lady" and "Looking On The Bright Side". Clint read each one's label before he threw, making a joke of it whenever he could. The others played up to him. A lot of giggling and craning of necks went into "Look Up and Laugh", for instance, while "Sing As We Go" got a howling cat's chorus.

Could Mr Archibald really sleep through this?

No problem, apparently.

Through record after record after record.

The last one of all was called "The Biggest Aspidistra In The World". "What's an aspidistra?" asked Moxie, handing it over.

"Pass," Clint said.

"A plant," I told them.

"You reckon? I expect it could do with some watering, then... couldn't it?"

Clint balanced the record on his fingertips. "Your choice, Skip. You want to destroy the old so-and-so's memories?"

I said nothing.

He launched it underhand like a discus. Turning in the air as if on an invisible turntable, the record floated the full width of the Quaggy, cracked sharply against the sewer pipe and slid gently into the river.

Clint sighed. "Well, that's the lot. Every one gone for a dip — and still not a dickybird from our Bob-a-Jobber here. Funny that... almost like these records didn't count, like they were finished with. Know what I mean? What's your opinion, Skip?"

"Haven't got one," I said.

"You're not fussed about it?"

"Not much."

"Really?" Clint said. "That's most peculiar... unless, of course, *this* is the explanation."

From his pocket he took a tape-cassette.

Even at this distance I could pick out Nimi's bold, clear writing on the label.

"Could this be why the records don't matter?" Clint went on. "It says 'Gracie Fields Medley' with a date from last week. Must be when you finished the job, Skip."

I felt sick. Why on earth had Nimi left the tape behind?

Panic probably.

Didn't I know all about panic? "Clint, I've been telling you the truth," I blurted.

"All of the truth?"

I hesitated. He saw this at once. "*All* of the truth, Skip?"

"Clint..."

My voice trailed away.

Clint whistled softly through his teeth. "Oh dear," he said. "What lonely last days that poor old git is going to have. And all your fault, Skip."

"No," I begged.

Delicately, between finger and thumb, he dangled the tape over the handrail. "Skip, think about it. Those records were practically historical, right? So there's no way he can replace them — unless he comes across another crumblie with his wife's taste in music. A bit doubtful that, wouldn't you say? Which makes this tape pretty important. Are you really going to make me dunk it?"

"No..."

"Talk, then."

"Please, Clint..."

"Ten seconds to decide, Skip. Starting now."

I didn't have to check my watch. I counted every second in heartbeats and hidden banknotes.

Finally, he let go.

The cassette hit the water sideways on, righted itself a moment as if it were going to float after all, then sank down and down into the weeds. "Pity," said Clint.

But it wasn't over yet.

Idly, he leant back on the handrail. We heard it creak under his elbows. "Know something, Skip?" he said. "I'm getting bored with all this. And I'm not the only one. My Little Friend is getting bored, too. In fact, My Little Friend's got her *snippy* feeling..."

The knife was back in his hand again.

I heard Moxie catch his breath.

Clint's eyes were on me. Mine were on the knife. Suddenly, with the same flick of the wrist he'd used on the records, Clint flipped it across the verandah like a dart. It hit the upright by my head so hard the woodwork shuddered, but maybe the angle was

100

wrong because it bounced back at once and clattered on the floorboards.

Instinctively, I kicked at it.

The knife skidded under the railings and dropped in the water. In the silence that followed a voice I barely recognized as mine said, "Tit for Tat."

"My knife..."

"And my cassette."

Olive, or perhaps Johnny Chan, gasped.

Clint's hand, still in its throwing position, fell slowly to his side. Just as slowly, he straightened up. "Clint?" Moxie warned him.

"Stay out of this."

"But Clint—"

"This kid is dead meat."

"Clint!"

"You heard me."

Only the glitter in his eyes mattered now. Being Clint, though, he couldn't resist one last taunt. Mimicking so perfectly that every TV-viewer in the land would've recognized the gesture, he pretended to flick back his hair.

That's when I snapped. I threw back my head and howled so loudly it sounded more like an animal than a kid. "REN!"

Ren! Ren! Ren!

Her name echoed high in the trees overhanging each bank of the Quaggy and faded into the city traffic. Clint's lip curled. "Scream as much as you like, Skip. You're still on your own. This is down to you and me — just the two of us. That sister of yours is out of it."

Moxie caught his arm. "Clint—"

"You heard me, Moxie. Naff off."

"But she's *not* Clint!"

"What?"

"She's not out of it. That's what I've been trying to tell you. Ren's over there—watching us."

"Ren?"

"Look!"

Moxie pointed.

She was so close I don't know how we could have missed her except, being Ren, if she'd wanted to be missed. Now she wanted to be seen. In her sun-yellow T-shirt, she stood in the exact spot where Nimi and I had first noticed Mr Archibald's house. The catapult dangled loosely from her hand. "Hi there," she said.

Her voice across the water was as clear as if she'd been with us on the verandah.

Only Clint could find something to say. "Still Babysitting, Ren?" he sneered.

"Still need it, Clint?"

"Your brother does."

"Doesn't look that way to me."

"No?"

"From here he seems short of space. That verandah's a mite overcrowded, Clint. Ricketty, too. Sure you can trust it?"

"Trust it?"

"To stay up," Ren said.

In slow motion, so none of us could miss what she was about, she raised the catapult, pulled the heavy-duty rubber from her outstretched fist as far as her earlobe, and took a sight high to our left. "Where's she aiming?" Johnny Chan asked.

"The rope, Dimbo," said Olive.

SNAP! THUD!

A puff of rope-coloured dust hung under the eaves. "Bullseye," said Moxie.

SNAP! THUD!

"And again," he choked. "Same place."

"It's got to be the same place," called Ren. "Don't you see? That's the trick. First you make a mark on the rope. Then you chip away at the mark till the rope starts to fray. Eventually..."

SNAP! THUD!

"Eventually," said Clint, "the rope falls apart and down comes the verandah. With your brother ending up in the Quaggy along with the rest of us. Forgotten that, had you?"

"No," said Ren. "Neither had Skip. Skip's always been quick on the uptake. That's why he's back at the door already — all set to nip inside."

"Right," I said, my hand on the doorknob.

"What's to stop us following him?"

"Me," said Ren.

"And the door after I've locked it," I added.

"He's right, Clint—" Moxie began.

"Shut your face."

Clint was thinking it over.

Before long he reached the question that had been bothering me. "So how do you expect *us* to get off this naffin' verandah?" he asked. "Fly?"

"Good idea," said Ren.

"What?"

She pointed. "See that patch of earth sticking out of the Quaggy? One good jump and you'll be on it. From there you can reach the bank."

"Impossible," Clint said.

SNAP! THUD!

"Clint!" Moxie yelped. "That's four shots smack

103

on target! How many can the rope take? We've got to do what she says — it's toxic, that water."

"Okay," sighed Clint.

He lifted his hands to show he'd surrendered... except he hadn't. His sudden spring towards me took almost everyone by surprise. The door shuddered in its frame as he crashed against it.

Safe in the house, I lifted the key.

I still have nightmares about Clint's face cussing and blinding through the glass, about his fingers clawing for me.

SNAP! THUD!

Shot Number Five was one too many for Moxie, Olive and Johnny Chan. With a terror that overwhelmed even their fear of Clint, they fell on him. He was dragged — screaming, kicking, swearing — back from the door. "Don't shoot!" they yelled. "Don't shoot!"

Even Clint realized it was over then.

Abruptly, he tore himself loose. His face blank, his eyes dead as a snake's, he brushed their contamination from his clothes with dainty, couldn't-care-less flicks. Nobody was fooled. Moxie, Oliver and Johnny Chan edged away from him, awestruck by what they'd dare do.

But they couldn't reverse it.

Ren had won.

By nightfall every kid in the neighbourhood, from the meanest back-double to the tallest tower-block, would be telling the tale of how Clint had been forced to back down. My sister was Queen of the Quaggy.

Of course, I'd known from the start she would be. Maybe Clint had, too.

CHAPTER · TWELVE

Clint didn't let losing cramp his style. Just as Ren had predicted, his first leap landed him nimbly on the island and his second took him to the bank.

The others weren't so lucky.

Moxie fell short with both jumps and had to drag himself, sodden and shuddering, from the water. Olive did better but still drenched her jeans. It was Johnny Chan who got stuck halfway and had to be lugged ashore by a sort of human chain.

I saw it all with my nose pressed flat against the glass in the French doors. Across the bend in the river, waist-deep in reeds, Ren watched their exit too — next to Nimi who'd come up behind her. Or had she been there all along? With Nimi it was hard to tell.

Were they waiting for me? I'd better get moving. But not before I'd checked with Mr Archibald.

Now the drama had passed, his house felt even more abandoned. For the first time I noticed the tick of an old clock buried somewhere under the dust-sheets. Even that seemed about to stop. Mr Archibald smiled gently as I bent over him. I heard the soft, rhythmic click of his teeth and noticed an eyelid twitch one or twice but otherwise he looked no more alive than a faded, dusty waxwork. "Mr Archibald?" I whispered. "I'm sorry about the records... and the tape. Was I wrong to save your money instead? We'll get some more Gracie Fields songs for you, I promise. Scouts' Honour, we will. We're bound to find some if we look hard enough."

Even as I spoke I didn't believe it.

Scouts' Honour?

Who did I think I was kidding?

I banged the front door so hard behind me the slam of it made my head ache as I ran. We were less than a catapult-shot apart but it still took ten minutes-worth of hard sprinting alongside the river, over the bridge, and back down the opposite bank before I reached the others.

Ren turned and smiled as I arrived. "Hi, Skip! Wasn't this kid here brilliant? She told me they'd all come shuffling outside to sink those old seventy-eights — because that's what she begged them *not* to do before she left. She sussed out the rope for me as well. It was her idea to convince them my catapult could snap it and dump the lot of them in the Quaggy. She's a genius, I tell you!"

"Nimi?"

"Didn't you realize she'd set them up?"

"No."

"Skip, there was no time to explain," Nimi said. "My main worry was to track down Ren — I knew she'd be somewhere close keeping an eye out for us. And I was certain you'd keep quiet about the money however much Clint bullied you."

"You were?"

"Of course I was. Even if he used his knife... which you kicked straight in the river. That was incredible!"

"Nifty footwork, Bruv," said Ren. "You know, by the finish of it I was half-expecting the verandah to collapse myself!" She was grinning from ear-to-ear.

So was Nimi.

I was grinning, too, though I wasn't sure why — especially when I saw how Ren gazed across the Quaggy again tap-tap-tapping the catapult against her leg like a charm to keep Clint away.

Or was it to bring him back?

She was in a Mum-type mood, I could tell. For her there was action still to come. " Reckon I should ditch this catapult?" she frowned. "Since you've got rid of Clint's knife, I mean? Doesn't seem fair to keep it now..."

"Ren–"

She lifted a hand to shut me up. She was only thinking aloud. My opinion had nothing to do with it.

Doubtfully, she twisted the catapult this way and that as if to view it from every angle. "I've been lucky so far," she said. "No living targets. But that can't last. Besides, Clint will never properly trust me while I've got this little beast up my sleeve. It gives me a permanent drop on him."

"Trust you?" I said. "Clint?"

"Clint, yes."

"You're still bothering about Clint?"

"Why not?"

"But Ren — he's damaged goods. And without the

107

catapult you can't be sure you'll go on winning. He may get the drop on *you*."

"Reckon so?"

She swung round to give me a wink. Or maybe to remind me it was her decision so any arguing was a waste of breath.

This was typical of Mum, too.

I gritted my teeth and said nothing. What was she up to now? Fumbling in her jeans for a pebble?

She found one, flipped the wrist-brace into position, pulled the heavy-duty rubber full length and lifted the catapult skywards. "Name Robin Hood mean anything to you?" she asked over her shoulder.

"The outlaw?" I said.

"That's him. Remember the last arrow he ever shot — how he wanted to be buried wherever it landed?"

"Yes."

" Well, if the worst comes to the worst, Skip... kindly do the same for me."

SNAP!

The pebble curved so high over the Quaggy and vanished so completely in the sun's midday dazzle, none of us had the ghost of a chance of seeing where it fell. That was the point, of course. Ren was giggling out loud as she lowered her weapon. Deftly, she wrapped it in its own elastic then balanced it on the flat of her hand. "Cheers, catapult!" she said.

The splash as it disappeared into the deepest part of the river came somewhere in size between a tape cassette and an old 78 record.

That was all.

Ren gave a long, low whistle of surprise. "What?"

she exclaimed. "No fist catching it like Excalibur? No swelling music or sudden thunderclap to make sure we don't miss the Big Moment? Stone me, Bruv... this might as well be Real Life! I'd better catch Clint up while things are *normal*. That okay with you? You've got your own catching up to do over in the house, I believe."

"That's right," I said.

"Take care, then."

"You too."

"Bye, Ren," said Nimi.

My sister blew us a final, jokey kiss. We watched the yellow blob of her T-shirt get smaller and smaller as she skirted the river and disappeared into the trees. Soon there were only trees to watch.

I sighed and glanced at Nimi. "Shall we go?"

"Not yet, Skip."

Her eyes were on the blocked-up sewer-pipe opposite. The noon sun picked it out so sharply against the murky water it had a strange, luminous look. "Skip..." she said.

"Yes?"

"There's... there's something else I must tell you."

"Go on, then."

"I can't, Skip. I'm too ashamed."

"Ashamed?"

I stared at her, baffled.

What was the matter with her?

She stood hunched and awkward, hugging herself with embarrassment. When she spoke, her words came in a rush. "Skip, it wasn't just Clint & Co. I set up. It was you and Ren as well. I should've told you everything right from the start, I realize that. I should've trusted you — especially when it was you who first suggested coming here. But I'd waited so long, you see. And I was so frightened. Even though I could hardly believe my luck, I didn't dare take the chance that you wouldn't understand *why* I had to check what happened, why I had to find out..."

"Find out what?" I asked

"About Ravi."

"Ravi?"

"Over there, Skip."

I looked across the river. "Ravi?" I said. "That was *Ravi*?"

She nodded.

When she spoke again, her voice was so soft I could barely hear it above the rustle of leaves and that dim murmur of traffic you never get away from in the city. "The house was so close, Skip. But so *spooky*. I didn't dare visit it on my own. But how else could I discover why no one there took any notice when Ravi must've been screaming, must've been calling for help..."

"So the trip to India..."

"Was a fib, Skip. Though we almost came to believe it, Mum and me. It made us feel better. In the end it was just easier to go on pretending, I suppose."

Slowly, I let out my breath. "Like my Bob-a-Job fib," I said.

We thought about this for a while.

Also, perhaps, about how little we still knew each other despite all that had happened.

Eventually Nimi said, "Skip... assuming it doesn't crop up and she doesn't actually ask, need Ren find out what happened to my brother? Can we keep it to ourselves?"

"Haven't you told her already?"

"I wanted to, really. For some reason I couldn't... it's just that Ren is so *tough*. She doesn't need fibs. Ren scares me a bit, Skip."

"Me too."

"You?"

"She scares me silly," I said. "I'm always petrified she'll want me to do something completely mad — such as taking a flying leap over the Quaggy. I'm just not like that."

"Neither am I."

We almost laughed with relief.

Finally, seeing there wasn't much we had to hide any more, we actually did laugh in a spluttery sort of way. I think we'd have stayed there for the rest of the afternoon, surrounded by all the tatty, citified wildness of the river, if we hadn't had a job to finish. "Got the tape?" I asked. "The back-up tape, I mean — the one Clint didn't know about?"

Nimi patted her back pocket. " Did you?" she grinned.

"Not till a moment ago when I remembered how tricky you are — and how you double-recorded everything."

"Just to be on the safe side, Skip. Or do I mean the bright side? Wasn't that his wife's favourite? Maybe it's the first one we should play Mr Archibald."

"Maybe we should play it for ourselves," I said.

I could hear it in my head already:

"I'm waiting for the right tide
And if luck comes to my aid
Giving me a break

I shall be awake
Looking on the bright side of Life."

It still sounded soppy.
But perky, too.
I took Nimi's arm. "Let's talk to Mr Archibald about the money," I suggested. "Let's tell him everything, okay? I've had it up to here with pretending."
"So have I," said Nimi. "Slap skin on it, Skip?"
"Slap skin," I said.
Even to a country kid, the crack as our hands met sounded good.